Johnny Westmore is a threat to everything Meredith has worked toward for years . . .

Johnny hesitated a moment, his eyes on her lovely profile. Then he tenderly slid his hand from her elbow up to her shoulder and turned her to face him. A sweet pink rush tinted her cheeks and made her eyes glitter as her gaze locked with his.

He swallowed tightly as his large hand gently held her face. She looked up at him, and he did what seemed the most natural thing in the world to do. He closed the short gap between them and gently kissed her.

Though the kiss was tender and brief, Meredith's mouth tingled, and all she could think of was that she wanted him to kiss her again.

No! Wake up! she thought wildly. In the space of a couple of seconds she'd forgotten all about flying and her school. Abruptly, she pulled away from him and opened the door. "Good night," she said, and hurried inside, as if she were fleeing from danger.

JANE LAMUNYON says she wrote her first inspirational romance because "I want to show that a fulfilling romantic relationship takes three persons: a man, a woman, and God." Jane is a wife, mother, and grandmother who lives in Southern California.

Fly Away Home

Jane LaMunyon

Heartsong Presents

A note from the Author:
I love to hear from my readers! You may write to me at
the following address: **Jane LaMunyon**
                                    Author Relations
                                    P.O. Box 719
                                    Uhrichsville, OH 44683

ISBN 1-55748-831-2

FLY AWAY HOME

Cover illustration by Brian Bowman.

one

Oh that I had wings like a dove! for then I would fly away, and be at rest.

Psalm 55:6

Meredith Bailey changed from her dress into her flying gear and pulled on her boots. She burst out of the small rest room, her hat in her hand, and grabbed a screw driver from her tool box.

"Jim, I'm going up. Turn my prop, please?"

The pilot looked up from between the wires of the strut he was working on and smiled at her. "Sure," he said and followed her out.

The sun was low, but she still had another hour or so of flying time. The September afternoon was humid, and the sky a pale blue as she and Jim walked toward her Curtiss Jenny where it waited on the grass beside the hangar. She gave the feminine little plane a loving pat on its lavender-hued side as she climbed into the cockpit. "It's just you and me, Birdie, old girl," she whispered.

Jim cranked the propeller, and Meredith adjusted the air pressure in the gas tank. When enough gas filled the pistons, Jim shouted, "Contact," gave the prop a final heave, and jumped back. The engine coughed and started, and Meredith taxied her plane down the grass, feeling better already.

The minute the wheels left the ground and she was airborne, a smile touched her lips. The exciting, wonderful feeling of being in the air was a sure cure for melancholy. She dipped the left wings and looked out at harvesting tractors moving slowly through the flat fields.

She gripped the control wheel then and nosed the plane up, concentrating on the last maneuver Tony had taught her before he'd left. She executed a perfect loop, did a couple of Immelman turns, flew along the train tracks, hoping to see a train, and then gave a sigh of pure pleasure.

Tension ebbed from her as she gazed at the dazzling white clouds shining ahead of her. The plane seemed lighter than air as she soared high above the ground.

This is joy unspeakable, she thought, remembering a Bible verse her father had made her memorize long ago. *Funny,* she mused, *I can't remember his sermons, but I can remember the Bible verses.*

The sun was dropping toward the horizon, so she turned back at last and landed. Walking back to the hangar, the free, joyful feeling of being aloft followed her like perfume.

Overhead lights were lit to banish the late afternoon shadows. Meredith sighed, suddenly lonesome for Tony. The only evidence his plane had ever even been there were some grease spots that resembled a map of Hawaii in the midst of a concrete sea. She hugged herself and looked away. *Being alone is nothing new. I'm used to it,* she thought.

She changed her coveralls in the rest room, putting on her dress, and said good-bye to the two men whose head were bent over the tail of the red Jenny they were repairing. The pungent smell of the dope used to glue the fabric followed her out the door.

She walked the mile to the boarding house where she lived. Inside, Mrs. Cooper, a tall, thin woman, knelt beside her new radio which had replaced her old crystal set. Turning the large knob, she said, "Paul Whiteman's on tonight," as proudly as if she knew him personally. Studying the dial, she added, "The young man's not with you, eh?"

Meredith sighed. Women of all ages noticed Tony. He'd come

home with her twice and entertained Mrs. Cooper at the dinner table. "No. He's gone to Omaha. It's just me tonight."

"Oh well." Mrs. Cooper's mouth puckered, but then she smiled with satisfaction as the room filled with music.

Meredith climbed the stairs to her small room. She pulled back lace curtains and watched an old couple slowly stroll through the twilight. Though Tony had tried to romance her, they had never been a couple. Now he had gone, and she missed him, but only as she would miss any friend.

But still, she no longer had any reason to stay in Nebraska. She had come here because Jim Lambert had advertised he'd teach *anyone* to fly, and since she was a woman, no one else would teach her. She had caught on quickly and even learned to do acrobat stunts.

Her eyes shifted from the window to the handbill she had tacked on the wall beside her bed. She had gotten the poster from a friend of Tony's who was leaving to join the air circus advertised in the picture: Meacham's Wild West Air Circus. The woman on the handbill was billed, "The Tomboy of the Air," and Tony's friend had said she earned five thousand dollars a month plus a percentage of the gate. Meredith had wanted to go with Tony's friend right there and then to California to join the circus, but Tony had persuaded her to stay. Now she wondered why she had let him. By now, Tony's friend would have moved on; even the "Tomboy of the Air" was probably no longer there, for Meredith knew that aviators were a restless bunch, moving from one job to the next. Because of that, she was certain she too could have found herself a job with the air circus.

She sighed, then squared her shoulders and went down to dinner.

That night she lay in bed thinking. She had long since reached her goal of learning to fly, and now she was merely biding her time, making a few dollars working as a mechanic for Jim. He had hired her on her merits, not biased by her gender, and she appreciated him for that. But she felt a restless urge to get on to the next stage of her life.

Her head filled with the familiar daydream of her own hangar. Over the building would hang a sign with large letters: BAILEY FLYING SCHOOL. She would never turn away a woman who wanted to learn, never.

She rolled onto her stomach, hugging her pillow against her. She was good enough to join Meacham's Circus to earn money toward that goal, she knew she was.

The next day she told Jim she was going to California. He slowly capped a bottle of dope and pursed his lips. "Not alone, I hope."

"Of course I'm going alone. Who would I go with?"

He shook his head. "You don't know what it's like out there. You and your Jenny came in on the train, remember? You've flown around here a bit, yeah, but that's different." He looked at her with troubled eyes. "A gal's got no place flyin' cross country on her own."

This was the most Meredith had ever heard Jim say at one time, and she was touched. "I'll be fine," she said brightly. "And before I go, I'll deliver the flowers for that wedding, pick up that package for you in Omaha, and do all the other errands you wanted."

"I'm not worried about that." He gestured with the brush in his hand. "Who's going to turn your prop while you're gallivanting cross country?"

She laughed. "I'll do it like everyone else does. I'll tie down the tail skid and crank the prop myself."

"Can't count on no regular landing field," he warned.

"I have a road map, and I'll stick close to the highways."

"Got it all figured out, huh?" Jim unscrewed the cap on the bottle of dope, stuck the brush in, and went back to work. She heard him mumble, "Women!"

For the next two weeks Meredith went up every day, practicing, trying new stunts, and fulfilling her obligations to Jim. At the end of the two weeks, she collected her pay, added it to her savings, secured her suitcases and blanket in the cockpit, her tools at her feet, and lifted off. Jim waved good-bye as she headed to California and Meacham's Wild West Air Circus.

She followed the Platt River west, then cut down south through Kansas, stopping in fields, sleeping under the wing some nights. Near the Oklahoma border she had to wait two days while a glowering storm passed overhead, venting its energy with sudden, steaming showers.

Back in the air again, she waved at school children as she passed over their playgrounds. She followed a train for a while, then stopped for gas in a four-corners town.

She landed in the field behind the gas station, then taxied up to the pump. By the time she'd filled the Jenny's tank, a crowd had gathered, surprised by the sight of a woman flying. Several took her up on her offer of five dollars for a ride, and she made enough to pay for gas for the next four days.

She went through the panhandles of Oklahoma and Texas so quickly she hardly noticed, and then she was in New Mexico. She figured that when she crossed the Rio Grande she'd be almost halfway to Los Angeles. But first she'd have to cross the mountains.

She crossed the Pecos River, landing in a small town near Roswell, where she saw some planes gathered near a large barn. A young man sauntered out to the makeshift runway, his eyes widening in appreciation when he saw her.

"What's a pretty little thing like you doing way out here all by your lonesome in this little flying plum?" His eyes swept from the lavender wing tip and then back to her face.

Meredith rolled her eyes and looked away. "Just passing through. I'm headed west. Which is the best way through the mountains?"

Three more men came out to meet the aviatrix of the delicately painted plane. They teased her and tried to flirt with her, but eventually they told her to head for Las Cruces where she could get through the pass.

She followed the river south to Las Cruces, gassed up again, then headed west. Though it was only September, the cool air became icy cold as she climbed steeply higher. She squinted at the mountain pass to the west, climbed still higher, and headed for the opening. Freezing wind pelted her face and numbed her hands in their leather gloves.

Suddenly, the pass angled sharply to the left. She gripped the control wheel and bit her lip. She had no room to turn around; with her fuel load she couldn't climb over the mountains that towered above her. Her only choice was to follow the winding pass.

"God, be with me and guide me," she whispered, her feet shaking a bit on the rudder, her eyes alert.

She wound around corners so steep she nearly stood the plane on its wings, until she was no longer sure which direction she was headed. She was up now to thirty-five hundred feet, and ahead she could see a gap between the peaks. But just below those peaks was a fog bank. Knowing she could not afford to become more disoriented, she flew over the fog, looking for a place to land.

Peaks surrounded her on both sides; the fog lay below. She studied her map and lifted to 4500 feet. Her jaw clenched, she leaned out and scolded the fog; she refused to turn back.

A violent wind hit the plane, hurtling her forward and upward like a dry leaf. She struggled with the control, keeping the sun to her left, the mountain peak to her right. The nauseating vapor of burning castor oil hit her as a thin ribbon of black smoke streamed past her face. She shivered, knowing she'd have to land soon.

Moving down to skim the top of the fog bank, she flew on,

keeping the sun ahead and a little to her left. She knew she couldn't keep the plane this high for long, and she continued northwest, looking for the end of the fog bank.

Finally, the white mist thinned, and she saw a deer bounding through the trees below and then a lake. She thought she saw enough space to land, so she quickly nosed down. She glided beside the shoreline, touched the ground, then hit a hole with her right wheel, dipping her right wing skid into the water. She nearly bounced out of her seat, but she managed to lift the wing quickly to avoid spinning into the lake, and finally rolled to a stop.

Ignoring her aching fingers, she struggled out to examine the damage. After the noise of the engine, she needed a few minutes before her ears adjusted to the quiet. When they did, she noticed the gentle lapping of the lake, the splash of a fish leaping out of the water.

She found a rip in the fabric, about a foot from the wing tip. Swallowing the queasiness in her throat and clasping her hands together against her chest, she closed her eyes and took a shaky breath. If the wing had gone another few inches into the water, she could have been stranded here, hundreds of miles from anywhere.

Her hands were shaking when she retrieved her wicker stool, a can of oil, her tool box, dope, and the extra linen strips she'd brought. She walked around the plane, checking everything, tightening screws, and then repaired the torn wing.

That night she decided not to sleep on the ground where bears or mountain lions might be prowling. Instead, she slept in the cockpit. Her sleep was shallow, disturbed toward morning by a wailing yowl from somewhere on the hill beside her.

When morning came at last, a heavy fog muted the sun's warmth. Meredith climbed out and stretched to relieve the chill and ache from being confined to the cockpit all night. She took a cookie from her knapsack and poured fresh lake water into her jar.

When she had eaten and drank her fill, she dug into her small suitcase and pulled out a small square package wrapped in her mother's lavender silk scarf. Tenderly, she unwrapped the fabric and took out her mother's Bible. Holding it gently, she sat down on the ground beside the plane and gazed out across the lake.

Her mother had always loved the water, and she had taken Meredith and her sister Pearl to the shore whenever Meredith's father had meetings in English seaside towns. Meredith smiled, remembering.

She was too young to remember the time when Pearl was born, but she had heard the story so many times when she was growing up that she felt as though she did remember. Her mother and father had told and retold the story of how hard they had prayed while the midwife had kneaded Pearl's still, cold chest, until at last God breathed into the tiny lungs, and Pearl gave a small wail of success. Cries of joy had heralded Pearl's entry into the world of the living.

Pearl had always been frail, though, but very lovely, and Meredith had both loved her and fiercely protected her. When Pearl and their mother had died, Meredith had been wild with grief. All the softness and light had gone from her life.

Now she squeezed her eyes shut to stop the tears that burned behind them, then stood and brushed the dust off the backs of her legs. She wrapped the Bible in its scarf again and put it away, wondering why she had gotten it out at all.

She filled her jar with water once again, then walked a long way beside the lake, carefully checking the ground, tugging large rocks out of the way. Grimacing back at the plane, she hoped for enough wind to lift her out.

At last she could put it off no longer, and she turned the plane around, then headed into the wind, bumping and scraping into the air with barely an inch and a half clearance over the trees. With her fuel gauge dropping, she landed an hour later at a gas station on the road near a ghost town by the Arizona border, her eyes blurring with tears of relief.

After that, the countryside changed dramatically. Gone were the dark greens and browns of the farms and fields of the midwest, replaced by a myriad of muted shades: mauves, tans, the dusty white dots of dry lake beds. The land looked hot down there, and she was glad to be up where the air was cool.

Finally, at long last, she reached Los Angeles. Using her map, she found the air show's field, then landed in a smaller field a few miles from her destination. She washed her face, put on her lavender silk jumpsuit that matched the plane, then took off again, heading for Meacham's Wild West Air Circus.

She circled, came in behind a Liberty Plane, and taxied to a stop. She was about to climb out of the cockpit when a deep voice full of authority startled her.

"What do you think you're doing?"

She looked down into the clearest blue eyes she'd ever seen, feeling as though they pierced straight through her, then watched them widen as he realized she was a woman. "I'm landing of course," she replied. He offered her a hand as she climbed out.

"This airfield is reserved for the show," he said.

She put her fists on her hips and smiled up at him. "You must be Jim Meacham." She extended her hand. "I'm pleased to meet you. I've flown a thousand miles for the pleasure."

He blinked. "A thousand miles?"

"Yes. I've come to be in your show."

Her green eyes flashed. He swallowed, then gestured to the grandstands behind him. "I'm not Meacham. That's him over there."

He looked down at the bright fire in her eyes and realized he was still holding her hand. He let it go and said, "I'm Johnny Westmore."

"Bailey," she answered. "Meredith Bailey. Pleased to meet you, even if you're not Jim Meacham." She flexed her fingers. "See you around, Mr. Westmore."

He looked from her airplane to her small form walking away, and a strange sensation of warmth washed over him. He shook it off, pulled his plane to its place beside the hangar, and forgot all about Meredith Bailey and her purple Jenny.

two

Meredith glanced around, breathing a sigh of pleasure when she saw that the field was clean, the bleachers orderly, and concession stands were boarded up, indicating that her timing so far was good. Getting a job here would surely bring enough money to open her school within a few months.

She smoothed down her wayward curls and tucked the sides behind her ears, glad she hadn't gotten it bobbed as Tony had suggested. She felt for stray hairs at the base of her neck and held her head up as she walked toward the grandstand to meet Jim Meacham.

Seated on the lowest bench, talking to a dark-haired woman, Mr. Meacham was dressed in baggy pants and a blue and white striped shirt. A straw hat lay beside him. With one foot propped on his knee he listened as the woman spoke with serious earnestness until she looked up at Meredith's approach.

He turned to see what had caught his companion's attention. His forehead went back to the top of his head, she saw, and his dark hair, combed down the sides, continued in sideburns around his chin and across his upper lip. He was smiling, and his grin lingered a moment for Meredith. "Can I help you, little lady?"

Meredith reached out her hand to him. "My name is Meredith Bailey," she said, "and I'm here to be in your show."

He laughed and clasped her hand. "You and a hundred others." He looked beyond her at her plane with a skillful eye. "What can you do, kid?"

"I do loops, dives, slow rolls, barrel rolls, and I've done Split-S and falling leaves."

"Sure. Like a dozen other barnstormers looking for work." His eyes narrowed. "What can you do that's different? Is there any stunt that is uniquely yours, that the audience has never, ever seen? Something no other aviator in the world can do?"

Meredith's jaw dropped slightly before she brought her teeth together and looked him in the eye. The question roared through her, and anxiety pounded in her ears. She must not let this chance escape. *Think fast.* The two words reeled themselves through her numbed brain.

The split second after his question before she answered seemed endless. Then she said, "Yes there is, and I'll show you."

He looked skeptical at her challenge and glanced at the woman beside him. "Fine. Helen and I will watch."

The woman smiled, the lines on the outer edges of her eyes deepening, giving her a kindly look. "Good luck," she said.

Meredith walked away from them with more confidence than she felt. She realized that all the stunts she'd done were standard; there was nothing she'd originated. Almost every possible trick in the sky had been done.

Then she remembered a stunt she'd heard about. She reviewed it in her mind, confident she could do it, because she'd mastered each of the parts. But never in that particular sequence.

Aloft in her plane, she circled the field, did a chandelle and a high loop, then held her breath. She nosed the plane up to almost four thousand feet, then plunged down to as low as a hundred feet before leveling out. She did another loop, flew between the grandstands upside down, turned, and landed.

A crowd of approximately twenty people crowded around her as she taxied to a stop near the hangars. Some were clapping their hands, and others were staring at her.

She climbed out, grinning, and looked right into the eyes of the aviator she had met when she arrived. He looked at her plane, then at her with an expression of disbelief bordering on indignation, then turned and walked away. She felt a little let down, but she kept on smiling at the crowd.

Jim Meacham approached with a stunned look on his face. "I won't lie and say I'm not impressed," he said. "But I don't want a suicide stunt in my show. Crashing and burning may be exciting, but in the end dead aviators scare people off. Sorry."

Meredith fought to keep her courage from faltering. "But I was in complete control." He shrugged his shoulders and started to walk away. "Mr. Meacham! I'll do it again, and you'll see—"

He stopped. The crowd watched closely. She wet her lips and waited. He looked over his shoulder at her. "You must really need a job." He fastened his gaze on her plane for a minute, took a frank and admiring look at her, then said, "If you're game, I think I can use you. Let's talk tonight, after the show." He walked away and the crowd disbursed.

Keeping her face from showing any emotion, she watched him, fighting the combination of triumph and disappointment that knotted up her stomach.

The woman named Helen laid a hand on her shoulder. "You scared us," she said.

Meredith looked up into a strong, tanned face with full lips, intelligent eyes, and dark hair pulled into two braids which were pinned to the back of her head. "Isn't that the idea?" Meredith gestured with palms up.

"Sure it is," agreed Helen, "but none of us thought you'd come out of that dive."

"But I did." Helen didn't answer, and Meredith repeated, "I did."

"Come on, let's tie your plane down. I'll show you around." Helen smiled, the lines radiating from her eyes suggesting that she laughed easily. There was a serene, regal quality and a sense of goodness about her that intrigued Meredith.

Together they pulled Birdie beside the hangar and tied her

down. Helen rubbed a dark hand over the violet paint. "Nice color. Do it yourself?"

"Yes." Meredith's disappointment clung to her. Somewhere in the hangar beside them a motor roared.

Helen motioned to the cockpits. "Let's get your gear out for now. You can stash it with my things." As if she read mistrust in Meredith's hesitation, she added, "Or maybe you'd rather be alone to wander around by yourself."

Meredith realized she could learn a few things about the Circus from Helen. She pushed her disappointment aside. "Thanks for the offer," she said. "And call me Merry."

"Good. Merry it is." Helen lifted the box from the rear cockpit, and Meredith reached in front for her suitcases.

True to her word, Helen introduced her to almost everyone and told her how Meacham's show worked. "Meacham's in charge of everything. Even the concession stands. This is *his* show, and what he says goes. He's fair, and he has an uncanny knack for knowing what will bring the crowds and keep them coming back.

"Sunday nights he has a meeting to review the shows and unwind. We've earned it after the exhausting work of risking our lives for the crowds' entertainment." She nodded before Meredith could reply, "I know, I know. But your stunt is too close to being certain death, and he won't risk that."

She showed Meredith her costume, made of soft tan leather, with a fringe hanging across the shoulders and a beaded headband. "I'm Navajo, and I'm billed as 'Dancing Eagle.'" Heavy silver and turquoise jewelry hung from a peg over the mirror beside a photo of Helen in her full Indian regalia.

At noon the concessionaires began opening their booths, and cars filled the dirt lot across from the entrance. A tall, auburn-haired man with a megaphone strutted in front of the bleachers, shouting of the death-defying stunts to come. Meredith caught the excitement, longing to be part of the show.

She stood beside the bleachers, watching the show open with an armada of eight planes swooping low over the crowd, the last two trailing long red banners reading MEACHAM'S WILD WEST AIR CIRCUS in bold black letters.

The show was unquestionably flashier than anything she'd ever seen. Helen "Dancing Eagle" was loved by the audience. They gnawed their fingernails while she stood spread eagle on the upper wing, gasped when she leaned out over the wing tip, slid down between the wings, walked along the lower wing, and slithered down the fuselage to hang by her knees from a bar between the wheels. The aviator swung the plane low over the crowd, and they shrieked as she let go with one leg, and seemed about to fall on them. She dropped a feather, and they scrambled to retrieve it as she was whisked up into the air.

Two aviators advertised as former war heroes did a mock air fight, complete with gunfire, which the announcer bragged was real, but which Meredith knew was not. The effect was stunning, especially when one plane dived to a field behind a nearby hill and an explosion and fire heralded its supposed defeat.

There were air races, with speeds over two hundred miles per hour, daring parachute drops with chutes which Meredith knew didn't always open, and "Loop Ace Clyde Turner" whose Jenny was similar to Meredith's, performing stunts she knew she could do.

The star, whose name was largest on the handbill, was Kate LaFore. Wearing white satin coveralls, she rode the top wing, sailing through the air as though she were in a genteel ballroom. With astounding grace and sure-footedness she cavorted across the wings, flashing smiles at the crowd. They turned white with fear, as the announcer warned of the force of the howling wind, and the propeller which could become a meat grinder if she merely slipped once. Kate laughed at the wind, waved her arms gaily and swayed her lovely body, and the crowd went wild.

The finale was a parachute race, and the first chutist to hit the ground won. Women swooned as bodies fell from planes and parachutes weren't opened until almost too late.

When it was over, people lined up to fly for a few minutes. The debonair war heroes with a grand flourish gave a scroll to their riders, proclaiming they'd assaulted the heavens with a flying ace. Dancing Eagle presented each of her riders with a feather attached to a small leather thong and colored bead. Kate LaFore's plane did not take riders, and she was nowhere to be seen.

Meredith passed customers lined up for rides, her head swimming with ideas of a hundred ways to make money, whether she worked with Meacham or not. Obviously, the public loved a show and would pay to be scared out of their wits.

She passed a sign saying "Westmore Aviation. Safe Transport for Business Trips, Vacations, Outings." A teenage boy pressed flyers into the hands of onlookers. The flyer claimed that the future of flying would not be in stunts, but as transport for the masses, for mail and goods, and invited the curious to take a closer look at his plane. Meredith walked on as the boy directed a man toward Westmore's DeHaviland.

Johnny stood beside his plane, his hand in the pocket of his loose black jacket, surrounded by gawkers. His eyes met Meredith's across the field, and she felt enveloped in a mysterious stillness. It stopped her for a few seconds, then she forced her gaze away from him and continued on her way.

She rounded the corner to where Birdie was tied down, and found Helen and her aviator in the shade, relaxing in wooden chairs, drinking lemonades.

Helen had removed her costume and was wearing a red dress with a black belt around her waist. "Hello again. Did you like the show? By the way, this is Joe." She nodded at the totally relaxed aviator slumped in the chair beside her.

"It was fabulous! You were terrific!" Meredith paced back and forth in front of them, unable to stand still with all the ideas racing through her head.

"Are you going to light somewhere? You're making me dizzy," said Helen.

"Helen, the crowds! We could do night stunts and gather more people!"

"Yes, but spotlights following planes are hard to manipulate."

"Sparklers!" shouted Meredith, over the roar of a plane taking off with its happy passenger.

"One little spark and you could go up, or down, in flames."

"I saw it done in New York. The plane had sparklers on the ends of its wings. It was beautiful!" Meredith clasped her hands and continued pacing. "They must have been special sparklers," she muttered.

"Get your ideas together, and we'll talk tonight." Helen rose, and looked down at Joe, who was asleep. "I'll meet you here at seven o'clock. Dress up if you can, and don't eat anything, there'll be a feast at the meeting."

So she wouldn't forget even one idea, Meredith jotted them on a scrap of paper. She hung her dress inside the hangar, then polished her plane until it glowed. She didn't see Joe leave, but he was gone when she finished.

She was wiping invisible specks from the wires stretched tautly between the wings, when her eyes lost focus and her hand slowed. She seemed to see a vision of those blue eyes looking at her across the field. They were eyes you couldn't forget. Eyes that seemed to look beyond the here and now, into a mysterious future.

She rubbed the wire quickly from bottom to top, feeling a little foolish. A lot of people had interesting eyes—so what? *Aviators are a faithless lot,* she sternly reminded herself.

Helen returned, and they went in her roadster to a mansion

nestled in the hills. They pulled the car up the drive and parked beside others already nosed in next to a tennis court.

The house looked like an English hunting lodge that could house the royal family easily. "Who lives here?" asked Meredith.

"The house belongs to a movie producer, an old friend of Meacham's." Helen smiled at her amazement. "He's always needing more recruits for his pictures, and he's nice to us."

"Did you see the movie *The Great Air Robbery*? It was a couple of years ago," said Meredith.

"Yes, I did. Some fabulous flying scenes." The door opened as though by magic as they mounted the steps. Soft music from somewhere inside floated toward them.

A gallant, dark-haired Mexican man bowed with a flourish, "Señoritas, welcome!" He glanced past them, then asked, "You have seen Señorita LaFore, no?"

"No," said Helen.

The man's dark eyes did one more quick scan of the front porch, then caught Meredith's in their softly dark depths. The jet black lashes surrounding them widened as he took a closer look at her. "Hola, bonita," he sighed, while taking her hand, then bent to kiss the back of it.

Helen put her hand over Merry's. "Are you the official greeter, Jorge?" she asked. "This is Meredith Bailey."

The dark Mexican eyes continued gazing at Meredith. "*Mi amiga,* welcome," he said.

Helen laughed, pulling Meredith into a room large enough to hangar two planes. Across from them, near a wall of open patio doors, was a four-piece band playing "Pretty Baby." The Circus people stood in small knots, or sat in the graceful antique chairs grouped together. Smoke rose as they puffed cigarettes and talked.

A few heads turned and shouts of welcome greeted them. Jim Meacham pushed his way through a swinging door and strolled toward them. He put an arm around Helen, and smiled at Merry. "You two look spiffy tonight. Come, fill a plate."

He led them to a table stretched along one whole wall. Meredith bit her lip to keep from gasping. She hadn't seen so much food in one place since the Fourth of July picnic in Nebraska. She picked up a plate, eager to make up for all the fasting and meager meals she had snacked on during her cross-country jaunt.

Johnny leaned against the fireplace, one elbow rested on the mantel, the other gesturing to make a point to Jake, an aviator. He caught a movement to his right, glanced in that direction, and saw her. She was dressed in something dark yellow, and even from a distance she exuded a life force that was arresting.

The hat she wore covered her head closely, her eyes beneath it full of fire and burgeoning life. The sense that she was about to do something special set her apart from everyone else in the room. She walked with an air of "Here I am, world; pay attention," and it was an attractive attribute.

Johnny forgot what he was saying, and looked blankly at the man before him, who didn't seem to notice the lapse. He tried to pick up the conversation, but he couldn't stop his eyes from glancing back toward the girl.

She and Helen stood, plates in hand, their backs to him. Helen looked like a mother hen next to the diminutive girl.

Meredith tried to be polite while choosing the most filling food she could without being piggish. As she reached for a drumstick, she had the odd sensation that she was being watched.

As though some invisible call had reached her, she turned and caught him looking at her. Johnny caught his breath at the curious glow in her eyes. He nodded absently and looked away.

Meredith spooned some aspic and olives onto the last empty spot on her plate, and followed Helen out to the patio. Conscious of the man at the fireplace, she looked back. He seemed absorbed, listening closely to his companion.

Johnny looked Jake right in the eye, concentrating all his strength on what the man was saying, but he couldn't shake his awareness of the girl's every move. Who was she? One of those crazy stunt flyers who thought nothing of life, facing death to titillate a crowd and make a few bucks. That much he knew.

But he sensed she was much more. Why did someone so young choose such a dangerous profession? Who, really, was she? Striving to give full attention, he listened to Jake talk of his plan to enter the King's Cup Air Race in England next summer.

In a few minutes the band finished their song, and Jim Meacham directed the drummer to do a drum roll, signifying that the meeting was beginning. Merry and Helen and the other patio diners came in, and the band rushed to the banquet table.

"I want to thank you all," said Meacham. "We dazzled and scared thirteen thousand people on Saturday, and ten thousand today. Next week they'll be looking for something new. Any ideas?"

The group's discussion grew serious. The instability and unpredictability of the airplanes was a constant risk, even without the elaborate tricks. Each week someone, usually Johnny, came up with a new tip to stabilize the aircraft.

Merry listened, waiting for her chance. Finally, she spoke up when someone mentioned performing a touch-and-go before the crowds, stirring up a cloud of dust.

"I used wing skids for something like that," she said. "I'd have a farmer attach a scarf to the top of a bush and I'd fly over and pick up that scarf with a hook attached to the skid."

Meacham eyed her and rubbed his beard. "Maybe," he said. "But I had something else in mind for you, if you're interested."

Meredith leaned forward, her eyes glowing. "Whatever it is, I can do it."

Meacham grinned. "I think the crowd would go crazy for an aerial strip tease."

Meredith backed away in confusion. "What?"

Kate stepped forward. "I've been thinking that would be a great idea, myself." She looked at Meredith. "My crowd would love to see me undress. But I'd wear a body suit so they'd only think I was undressed."

Meredith's cheeks burned as Meacham looked from Kate to her, shaking his head. "No, Kate, you're the ballerina. I'd like you to enlarge your repertoire, but we'll discuss that in a minute. Our new girl here wants to be a part of the show, and with a strip tease, she'll get a lot of attention." The men loudly agreed with him.

"I'm an aviator," protested Merry.

"Precisely," he said. "You'll take off, do your loops and curves, and drop pieces of your wardrobe in front of the crowd. When you land, they'll be straining for a glimpse."

"I can't do that!" protested Merry.

"Do you want to be a part of my circus?"

"Yes, but . . ."

"Then you perform this act."

Merry licked her lips. "No. It would jeopardize my career," she said softly, disregarding the sudden silent attention focused on her.

Meacham eyed her skeptically, then said, "Stunt flying isn't your career?"

She felt all the eyes in the room on her. "Yes, but . . ." She swallowed hard, trying to quell her embarrassment. "I'm not that . . ." She bit her lip. She almost said she wasn't that kind of girl.

Meacham waved her objections aside. "We'll discuss this later." He looked over the crowd and settled on Helen. "What's your new trick for next week?"

Meredith studied her hands which were clutching each other

in her lap. She'd made the only decision she could. Barnstormers were known for doing anything for a thrill, but for her there were limits.

Johnny, standing off to the side, studied her profile. Her face seemed pale, but her chin was up. Her skill was amazing, but this came as a bigger surprise. Meacham was obviously surprised, too, by the way he quickly changed the subject.

The meeting was soon over, and the group gathered in small knots to discuss the next week. Meredith felt at loose ends. What was she to do now? Her savings wouldn't last long if she couldn't get work. She sighed, thinking she'd have to barnstorm California fields, unless she could come up with a better idea.

Helen touched her arm and said, "I don't know whether to sympathize or congratulate you."

Meredith shrugged. "It was the only decision I could have made. Who'd take a strip teaser seriously when considering a flying instructor?"

"There are many ways to appear to do something without really doing it," said Helen.

"Not for me," answered Merry. "Even the appearance of doing it goes against everything I believe."

The band began their preparations to play, and from somewhere bottles of bootleg liquor appeared on the table. Meredith decided to leave, but not before making one more effort to talk with Meacham.

three

When the booze began to flow, Johnny stood, leaning against a wall, staring after Meredith, still unable to keep his eyes off her. He tried to analyze what was happening, but she caught at something deep inside of him that was beyond reason.

Jorge walked by, a glass in his hand. "She's a hot number, eh?"

Irritated by his tone, Johnny pushed himself from the wall. "I've got things to do." He threaded his way through the knots of people and paused with his hand on the door.

He'd always left as soon as the business was over, and he was annoyed with himself for staying this time. Even so, he didn't open the door and go. He stood, the disturbing thought pressing him that he should go back and make sure the girl was all right.

"The girl." She'd told him her name: Meredith. He said it quietly to himself, liking the sound of it. At the doorway into the salon, his eyes unerringly found her.

She was looking up into Meacham's laughing face. But she wasn't smiling. She was gesturing with her hands to make a point, and every curve of her body radiated defiance. Meacham caught Johnny's eye, and motioned him to join them.

Meredith rephrased her words to Meacham. "With the air coming under the wings like this . . ." She wanted to grab him and make him pay attention. But he was looking away.

The man whom she'd been noticing all evening joined them. She drew a deep breath and pretended he wasn't there. But Meacham extended his smile to the man, including him in their conversation.

"Westmore," he said, "the little lady here wants to do some things I don't think her little Jenny is capable of."

Johnny looked down at her. Her face was animated with determination and enthusiasm. "I can do them! Come any day and watch. See if I don't give you a show you'll never forget."

Meacham explained one of the tricks to Johnny. "No plane can do that."

Johnny rubbed his chin. "Anything is possible, but . . ." He didn't want to help flying fools kill themselves outdoing each other in more and more dangerous stunts.

Meredith had to tip her head back to look up into his eyes. He had that far off look again. "But what?"

"But planes have limits. No matter how skilled the aviator is."

Meacham's eyes narrowed. "You're right. I think a Jenny would be more stable and have better maneuverability if the wings were reversed. Put the bottom wing on top."

Merry's heart sank. "But I know my plane, like a part of myself! It doesn't need . . ."

Johnny felt the room dim a little as her smile faded. He wanted to see the bright fire of her confidence flare again. "Before she goes into serious alterations, why not let her show you what she had in mind?"

"She almost killed herself this morning showing me what she had in mind."

Meredith began to feel annoyed that they discussed her as if she weren't there. "Mr. Meacham," she said, "I was never in danger this morning. I am in complete control when I fly. And Mr. Westmore," she fixed Johnny with her most assertive look, "I'm aware of the exact limitations of my plane."

"Fine," he said, wondering what he'd said to annoy her.

Meacham grinned at Johnny. "Maybe you're right. Let's see what she can do." He gave Meredith the smile of a benefactor. "Be at the field Friday at noon." He was already turned away from them, and a few steps took him into the crowd.

Meredith put her fists on her hips and watched him walk into the bluish smoke. "I'll show him!" She lifted her chin, meeting Johnny's bemused gaze with her defiant one. "At least he didn't insist on that dumb act he demanded earlier." The smoke made her eyes sting. "I've got to get outside and think," she said.

Johnny cupped her elbow, and they went out into the cool night air. They walked down the stone steps that curved around the house between dark shrubs and trees.

Merry thought about her depleted savings in the small bag at the bottom of her suitcase. The days until Friday would use up too much of her money. "I hadn't thought it'd be so hard to get into the Air Circus," she said.

Johnny stopped before a stone bench. "How old are you?" he asked, motioning her to sit. She was small and slender, but her figure was womanly.

"My age has nothing to do with this," she said, turning her head from him and sitting.

"You're right," he said, dropping down beside her and facing her. "I just wondered why a—why you do what you do. I mean, you seem young, and have so much to look forward to." He looked up into the dark trees. He'd almost called her a lovely young woman, and wasn't sure how she'd take that. He resisted the urge to look at her again. He didn't need to verify her loveliness.

Meredith looked up at his profile, dark against the moonlight. There was an inherent strength in his face. His hair was almost black, and she was glad his soul-piercing blue eyes were not focused on her.

She didn't answer him right away. She'd been asked this question before, but always in derision. He sounded sincerely interested, and she was taken aback.

Johnny waited calmly for her answer. The bench in the darkened garden seemed to have a modest intimacy that encouraged confiding in each other.

Meredith pushed herself to a standing position and looked up into the leafy darkness. "It's simple. I love to fly," she said quietly.

He forced his thoughts back past the horrors of war and its frightful experiences, to when he'd first learned to fly. It was a heady experience for a young man, barely more than a boy. He understood how she felt. "Mmmm," he murmured. "There's no feeling like it."

"Yes! The second the wheels leave the ground I get a little burst of happiness. The higher I get the more it grows. When I fly I feel as if I'm floating. Sometimes I think if I can turn my head fast enough I'll catch a glimpse of an angel. It's so sacred and pure up there, I . . ." Warmth crept into her cheeks, and she was glad for the semidarkness that hid her embarrassment. She'd been caught off guard by his soft voice, and now she felt she'd said too much.

He smiled and leaned forward, and as their eyes met she briefly looked away. He said, "I like the feeling of power and control. As if I can do anything—fly to the moon if I want. The thrill of doing something that for centuries mankind only dreamed about." He looked beyond her as if seeing a dream she couldn't even imagine. "And we're only at the beginning of a fantastic future no one can foretell."

She wanted to ask him about his dreams of the future, but little warnings darted through her thoughts, and she took a deep breath and said, "You're probably right." She turned to go. "I should get back. Helen will be looking for me."

He took her arm and they walked up the path. "You can bring your plane to my shop and work on it any time you like."

"Thanks, but Birdie isn't an experimental plane. I'll think about extending the bottom wing a few inches, which should test Meacham's theory." As they walked away from the cozy bench and left off personal talking, her apprehension melted.

Johnny stared at her for a moment, then burst out laughing. "You're an independent little lady!" he said.

She regarded him with a speculative gaze. "Yes. So?"

"You fly out here all alone, march right up to Meacham and announce you're here for the show, then refuse to do what he asks."

She stopped and looked at him defiantly. "He wasn't asking for flying expertise."

Affected by her wide-eyed innocence, Johnny's grin sobered. "True. He was out of line, and you did the right thing."

He walked slowly beside her, thinking about her bravery, delaying the moment when they'd be back at the house. "So, what are you going to do?"

"Think about each trick I saw today, make my own unique routine, and Friday I'll show him." She shrugged, as if she hadn't a worry in the world, but she was still disappointed Jim Meacham didn't seem to have confidence in her abilities.

They stood at the bottom of the sweeping steps leading to the house. Sounds of a party in full swing drifted out the open door.

Meredith hoped Helen was ready to leave. "Well, thanks for the kind words. I've got lots to think about, and a lot to do to get ready for Friday." She reluctantly started up the steps. She wasn't usually shy, but tonight she felt out of place in the party atmosphere.

"Where are you staying?" Johnny asked.

"With Helen," she said, looking back at him.

"We're neighbors," he said. "I'd be glad take you home, but . . ."

She glanced at the lighted window, and saw the burning tip of a cigarette. "Thanks! I'll go tell Helen," she said, before he could finish his sentence and tell her why he couldn't take her.

He rested his arm on the concrete ball which topped the pillar at the bottom of the steps and took a deep breath of the strong flowery smell surrounding him.

She came out a minute later, pulling off her hat. Her hair sprung out in golden waves around her face. She reached up with one hand and swept them back. He wished she hadn't done that. He liked the vision of her coming toward him with her hair loose. He was sorry he wouldn't be taking her with him.

He led her through the autos filling the parking area, to a group of motorcycles, most looking as though they hadn't seen soap and water in months. He stopped at the only one whose blackness actually gleamed in the moonlight.

"You didn't say you were riding a motorcycle."

"I didn't get the chance," he said.

She glanced at her skirt and slipped the ribbon of her silk purse up her arm. "Sidesaddle, it is then," she said, but he slowly shook his head.

"Not possible. You'd be off center. And your dress could get burned on the exhaust."

Mentally, she chastised herself for her impetuous insistence on going home now, but he could have told her he had a motorcycle. Now, how long would it be until she got home?

"I have an idea," he said. "Wait here."

She stood among the motorcycles, in her yellow dress, clutching her purse, while he moved through the cars like a shadow.

He came back carrying a bundle. "Curley's coveralls," he said, tossing them to her. "If you want to get home before the wee hours of the morning, this is your only chance." He gave her a smile which challenged her daredevil attitude.

She looked at the coveralls in her hand, scanned the area for a private place to change, handed him her purse, and walked into the bushes.

"I'll stand guard," he called after her, grinning in spite of himself at her spunky attitude. He started to laugh out loud when she emerged with her dress draped over her arm, the arms of the coveralls in huge rolls at her wrists and ankles. But his amusement quickly died when he saw the warning in her eyes.

He took her dress, folded it, and put it in front of him. She climbed on behind him and gripped the side of the seat. He twisted around and took one of her hands, placing it around him, then did the same with the other. "Hold on to me tightly. We have to be a unit. Lean when I lean—and relax."

She hung onto him as they bounced over the narrow road down the hill to the street. He felt strong and warm. She hadn't noticed how broad his shoulders were, until she tried looking around them.

His hair, blowing back toward her, looked silky. "Here we go!" he said, as they turned onto the highway. She felt the deep vibrations of his voice as he spoke, then the motorcycle surged with power. Though the wheels skimmed the road, she felt like they were flying. They sped through the night toward the ocean.

He slowed when they reached Venice, cruising through the dark streets to the apartments.

Meredith had enjoyed the exhilarating ride, but holding on to him so tightly, feeling his warmth and strength, was beginning to make her nervous. When he stopped, she quickly released her arms and slid back a few inches.

He got off, then she did, saying, "Thanks for the ride." She reached for her dress and purse.

"My pleasure." He handed her the bundle and grinned. "Yes, you are one independent little lady."

She wasn't sure if he meant that as a compliment or not, so she decided to say nothing.

"Well, good night," he said, wheeling the motorcycle toward the side of the front apartment.

❧

Monday morning she left the coveralls at his front door, and after practicing, she spent a few dollars from her stash on a small amount of wood and fabric. She worked at Meacham's field, trimming wood, shaping and adding a few inches to the lower wing.

Johnny's business kept him busy, transporting passengers to San Diego on Monday morning, back again that afternoon; then on Tuesday he delivered tools to a garage in the desert and brought back a puppy. Between flights, he and his mechanic worked installing a larger motor in a DeHaviland, and reconstructing a crumpled Sopwith that hadn't cleared the telephone wires at the end of a local runway.

Busy as he was, his thoughts kept straying to a lively little strawberry blonde who had literally flown into his life. He kept seeing her striding confidently to meet Jim Meacham the day she arrived. He seldom dreamed, but lately when he awoke he began to sense he'd been dreaming. Then he'd think of her, and wonder what she was doing. He'd frown, thinking she was most likely feverishly devising life-threatening stunts for her big audition Friday.

Merry was working hard. She had met the milkman and found that Helen's home was one block from the end of his run, so she talked him into taking her down Main Street close enough to the air field so she could walk the rest of the way. That saved a few cents on the way in to her plane

On Wednesday the good weather gave way to large, dark clouds. She glowered up at them saying, "No! Not today. Not this week! Go away!" It couldn't rain before she finished her work. The dope needed to dry, and she had to test the results before Friday.

❧

That afternoon when Johnny taxied in after his last trip, his nephew was there to meet him. The fat, golden puppy scampered around his heels. "Chad! Have you been here long?"

The ten-year old looked at his uncle with open admiration. "'Bout twenty minutes. Mom dropped me off. She said I could help you a while before church."

Johnny grinned and gave the boy's hat a half turn, then reached down to the wiggling puppy, who licked his hand. "Ace here was good company yesterday. What do you think of him?"

Chad knelt and scratched the pup's head. "He's terrific!" He looked up at Johnny. "He's an ace, all right."

"You can call him anything you like. He's yours, if you want him."

The boy's eyes widened and his mouth dropped open. "Dad—"

"Said it was okay. I checked with him first."

Chad stuck close to Johnny, running to put the rope back on its nail, bring a bit of wire, and doing whatever else he could to help. The pup was close on his heels. Ernie, the mechanic, laughed out loud when Chad almost stumbled over the frisky dog, and Curley filled a bowl of water for him.

That night in church Johnny sat beside his brother and his family. Nate and Edith had three wonderful children, and Johnny loved them. Nearly six months ago he'd asked God for a helpmate of his own, but nothing had happened yet.

The congregation stood and sang "Rock of Ages," their voices flowing around him. Couples and families in the first few rows raised their voices together. Behind him Mrs. Cleveland, a widowed lady, looked up as if she could see God as she sang the familiar words.

The song ended and the pastor asked for prayer requests, and Johnny added his own silent, . . .*remember my prayer, Lord, for a life partner, a helpmate.* While they were praying for the various requests, a joyous, elated feeling washed over him. Then Meredith's smiling face stole into his thoughts.

I don't understand. He could still feel the elation, and he felt

God smiling at his inability to understand something very obvious.

Her? Oh, no, Lord, she's not the type I had in mind. He felt God still patiently smiling. *She's a daredevil! She risks her life for a few dollars! Not exactly wife and mother material. Maybe she's not even a Christian! Maybe I'm imagining this, and it's not really You speaking to me?* Even as he voiced his objections, he felt God's satisfaction, and he knew his prayer was answered. He felt he should be grateful, yet he was puzzled at the choice. He'd expected someone more like his sister-in-law.

His mixture of gratitude and puzzlement stayed with him all evening. The next morning he awoke with a smile, then noticed the sun wasn't shining. He lifted the shade and saw black clouds threatening a downpour.

Meredith's plane was not inside a hangar. He wondered if she was finished working on it. After reading his daily Bible chapter and praying, he couldn't suppress a grin as he skipped breakfast to jump on his motorcycle to dash to Meacham's airfield. It was time to get to know this Meredith Bailey.

four

Meredith painted a line of dope across the wood. She stretched linen over it, glancing up at the dark sky. "Just a few more minutes," she muttered to the threatening clouds.

She heard a motorcycle, and thought about Johnny: his sky-colored eyes, the straight lock of hair that fell over his forehead, and the warmth she felt as she rode behind him.

She jabbed the brush into the can, willing her thoughts back in line. He might not do stunts, but he was an aviator, which meant that somewhere underneath his calm exterior lay a conceited, pushy person, like every other aviator she'd ever met.

The motorcycle roared closer, and she looked through the wires. It was him. She closed her eyes, quelling the surge of happiness that nudged her heart, and refused to look at him again.

He coasted closer, switched off the motor, kicked down the stand, and stood for a moment watching her. She leaned over the wing tip, tugging fabric over the wooden frame. He knew she heard him approach, and wondered why she didn't acknowledge him. *Maybe she's one of those persons who gets lost in her work,* he thought.

Walking toward her, he felt a drop of rain on his head and glanced up. The damp air intensified the pungent smell of dope. "Good morning," he said.

Meredith pursed her lips as dark spots began to dot the linen. She tried to shield it with her arm. "Lovely," she said, gritting her teeth in irritation.

He went to the hangar and peered inside. Two planes filled it. "You must get inside." He admired her zealous work, but she couldn't beat the rain.

She looked at him as though he were too dense to understand anything. "There's no room in there," she said, and bit her lower lip hard to keep from giving in to defeat. She'd have to cover the work with oil cloth, and wait out the rain, then continue later.

He slid open the hangar door enough to slip through, and came out with half a bed sheet, which he tore into strips. "Here, let's wrap it and take her to my hangar."

He quickly began winding strips around the wing frame, as though bandaging a broken arm. The rain was still sprinkling softly, and she tightly wrapped strips beside his.

When they were sure the patch was secure enough for flight, he rolled his motorcycle into the hangar and helped Meredith push her Jenny onto the airstrip. He cranked the prop and climbed into the front cockpit. They took off and flew the ten miles, with Johnny shouting directions back to her. The sprinkles turned into serious raindrops as they taxied down his airfield.

Johnny raced for the hangar, opened the doors, and helped Merry pull Birdie inside.

"Thank you very much, but what were you doing at the field this early in the morning?" She whipped a rag from her back pocket and wiped the tail gear, ignoring the streams of water running from her hair down her neck.

"Looking for you. I knew you'd be outside working, and when I saw the clouds—" he shrugged, "I knew you'd need a dry place to work." He extended his arm and motioned through the hangar. "There's plenty of room."

"Yes." She was pleased at the warm, dry hangar, but not happy with the fact that it was his. She'd hoped to avoid seeing him, and she didn't know what to say. She pressed her coveralls to her neck to soak up the drips running down her back, and leaned sideways, grabbing her hair and giving it a shake.

Johnny watched in fascination. She looked like a child, and he felt a surge of protective feelings toward her. He saw her confusion, and wondering if she were suddenly shy, he said, "Well, I've got work to do, so I'll leave you to your devices. The toolbox under the DeHaviland belongs to Ernie." He pointed to the middle of the back wall. "Those are mine. Feel free to use whatever you need."

He went over to the broken Sopwith and hunkered down beside the wing lying on the floor beside it.

Rain pounded the roof while Merry unwrapped the soaking strips and set about finishing her wing extension, pausing periodically to look around the spacious hangar. It was clean and organized. The cool damp air intensified the scent of dope mingled with the wood and oil smells from the planes.

She heard an occasional car drive by and wondered how Johnny was going to get around without his motorcycle. He was definitely not a safe subject for thought, judging by the happy feeling that had welled up when she saw him earlier. She determined to keep such feelings from happening again.

There was something about him, though. Maybe it was the way he looked at her, as if he could see straight into her heart's hidden corners. She shook her head slightly and continued working. Maybe it was just the fact that he was good looking, and his chest felt rock hard and strong when she was clinging to him on the back of his motorcycle.

Stop that, she said to herself. *Looks mean nothing.* Her traitorous eyes glanced at him, but she crossed her arms firmly over her chest and forcefully ejected him from her thoughts.

A few minutes later Ernie came in with coffee and warm cinnamon rolls, and Johnny introduced him as "the man who could fix anything that flies, drives, or moves by motor." He was of medium height, and blonde, with a small mustache. Meredith liked him immediately.

Johnny felt as if a ray of sunshine lit up the darkness when she smiled at Ernie and held out her hand. She'd disarmed him last Sunday with that same radiant smile when she arrived and thought he was Meacham.

They had the coffee and rolls, talking about planes and when the rain would let up, and then they each went back to work. Johnny took off to run a few errands.

The rain continued all day, with a mere fifteen-minute interval of drizzling sunshine. Meredith blew on her work, willing it to dry faster. She cleaned each wire, stroked and rubbed Birdie's every square inch, and checked regularly to see if the rain was lessening.

Johnny returned later to find her going back and forth to the doors, peering out, as if hearing the rain on the roof wasn't proof enough that it was pouring.

Curley came in, saw her, and grinned from ear to ear. "A lady mechanic! And she's a keen looker!" Meredith concentrated on her work, and Johnny pointed the lad to his chores.

Finally, when twilight darkened the square of light filling the door, Johnny turned on the overhead lights. He strolled over to her, wiping his hands with a rag. He wanted to tell her he was sorry about the weather, but he was afraid she'd only feel worse. He glanced from her to the door. "Someone wore a path in the floor between here and the door."

At first she started to object, then realized he was merely trying to lessen her tension. "I hoped to get up for at least fifteen minutes."

"The storm will pass, and tomorrow will be better."

She had to smile at that. "Promise?"

There was that smile he'd thought about all day. "Absolutely," he said, determined to see that she relaxed after her disappointing day. "You must be starved. I am. How about dinner?" He grinned. "Or would you rather eat here in case the rain lets up a minute before it's pitch black out there?"

She laughed. "Was it that obvious?"

"Like I said, there's a path between here and the door."

Ernie dropped Johnny off at Meacham's field so he could pick up his motorcycle, then took Meredith to the apartment.

She ran inside to change clothes. Helen sat at the kitchen table, sewing beads onto her headband. She held her needle poised and smiled easily. "Ahh, Little Sister, you're home!"

Meredith picked up a blue glass bead and looked through it. "I'm going out to dinner, so I only came in to change."

"Dinner!" Helen's brows rose quizzically. "With the milkman? Who else do you know?"

"No, silly! The milkman's old enough to be my grandfather." She dropped the bead back into the ornately painted tin. "Mr. Westmore," she said, "and I only have a few minutes to change clothes."

Instantly alert, Helen set the headband down. "Johnny Westmore?"

"Yes. Our neighbor, Johnny."

"Landlord Johnny, you mean." Helen gave her a thoughtful look. "I've never seen him interested in anyone—and dozens of women have tried to impress him." Her eyes narrowed. "Hmm."

"We just work together," said Meredith, turning to leave.

"Yes, of course," said Helen in a tone which said she didn't believe it for a minute.

Johnny had said they'd use his car instead of the motorcycle, so Meredith selected a simple white linen blouse and a long, close-fitting light blue skirt, to make her appear taller. Helen stood in the doorway. "He's a quiet one, but I think there's a lot beneath that cool, aloof surface."

Meredith sniffed at the obvious attempt at matchmaking. "It doesn't matter one way or the other," she said, cinching a belt around her waist. "Did you say he's our landlord?"

"Yes! He owns these apartments." She was about to say more when a knock sounded on the door.

Meredith pulled her hair back with tortoise shell combs and took a last close look at her face in the mirror.

She almost tripped over the small rug in the living room doorway at the sight of Johnny Westmore. He wore a striped shirt and dark pants, with that same black jacket he'd had on at the party, casually draped over his shoulder. Small droplets glistened on his dark hair. She opened her mouth to speak, but nothing came out. He looked like an ad in *Vanity Fair*.

Johnny smiled in approval. She stood there, her small size speaking of vulnerability, belied by that inner strength that seemed to sparkle though her. "You'll need an umbrella."

Helen picked up a magazine from the pile near the sofa. "Here, use this," she said.

They ran between the one-story apartments, to Johnny's Maxwell, and he settled her inside.

"I know a great place in downtown Los Angeles," he said, turning onto the deserted street. "Next time, when it's not raining, we'll motor through the new Mulhullond Drive. The view is almost as good as you'd get from the cockpit."

She settled back, vowing there'd be no next time, and wondered how she let herself get into being alone with him tonight when she'd decided to keep her distance. Determined to keep the evening on a friendship level, she crossed her arms and enjoyed the warmth of the car as it rumbled along the narrow streets past dark, drenched orchards and houses with glowing windows of light.

Downtown he parked the car near a row of shops, and they ran through the rain to the restaurant.

"I hope you like Mexican food," said Johnny, taking the soggy magazine from her, and laying it beside the umbrellas standing near the door. A row of empty chairs lined the wall.

"I never ate any," she said, admiring the huge sombrero hanging on the wall beside a colorful serape. From the round arched doorway came a beautiful dark-haired woman wearing a white blouse and brightly-colored skirt. *"Comida para dos?"* Johnny nodded. "Theese way," she said, her skirt whirling around her legs in a blur of color as she led them into the restaurant.

Meredith felt like she'd stepped into a foreign country. The candle-lit dimness reminded her somewhat of the eating establishments in England. But the spicy, tart smells here were like nothing she'd ever experienced. Instead of Victorian decor, the walls were decorated with Mexican art work on whitewashed walls. Standing in the corner, two guitarists strummed softly.

Johnny ordered for them, then inclined his head toward her, enjoying the innocent pleasure in her eyes. He wanted to get to know her, and especially to find out if she were a Christian.

He decided to start with a safe subject which they'd discussed before. "So. What brought you into the world of aeronautics?"

She looked upward, remembering. "My Aunt Lulu took me up in a balloon when I was eight. We floated over the English countryside like a feather in the breeze, and I was utterly fascinated. For years after that I dreamed of going aloft, and when I accumulated enough money to go up in an airplane, I knew I must fly one myself."

The waiter brought a plate of wrapped tortillas and a dish of red sauce. Johnny picked one from beneath the warm napkin, rolled it up, and dipped it into the sauce. She imitated him, and her eyes flew open in shock. She reached for the water and gulped frantically.

"I'm sorry," he said. "I forgot to tell you to go easy on the sauce."

She wiped moisture from her eyes and drew deep cooling breaths. When she could finally speak, she asked, "What brought *you* into the world of aeronautics?"

"I was just a city kid from Cincinnati when the war broke out, but when the call went out for men to join the air force and go overseas, I was one of the first to sign up. I went to France, an exciting place for a boy who'd never been more than a few miles from home. I was assigned to an English squadron near the front, and literally learned to fly by the seat of my pants." He didn't mention the painful scenes of combat, the despair, and useless loss of young lives.

He looked across the room for the waiter, and Merry wondered what caused the deep lines of sadness that suddenly appeared between his eyes.

The waiter came, and Johnny requested a pitcher of water. "Where did you get your Jenny?" He asked her, wondering if she was one of the rich who bought planes as amusing playthings.

"In New York. I went to secretarial training school there. On weekends I worked odd jobs to earn money to go to air shows, and I talked to lots of people. When I graduated, I worked two jobs, finally saved up the three hundred dollars to buy a surplus Jenny."

"So then you learned to fly."

"Not as easy as that," she said, shaking her head slowly. "Because I'm a woman no one would teach me, so my plane sat in its crate for two months until I got enough saved up for train fare to Nebraska. It cost more for the plane than for me."

"Why Nebraska?"

"Because I heard there was a man there who'd teach anyone to fly—even a woman."

"Did he teach you stunts?"

"No!" Meredith poured water from the pitcher into her empty glass. She didn't even want to think about Tony. Unless it was to remind her not to become too friendly with this charming man.

Raising his glass to his lips, Johnny sensed her withdrawal. "Who did?"

"A local aviator," she said, willing herself to keep the subject light. "Have you ever done stunt flying?"

"If you can call wild maneuvering to stay alive when the deadly Fokkers are on your tail." He shrugged. "I see no other reason to push an airplane and a life past its limits."

Meredith hadn't expected the barb at her career. "It's a living," she explained. "And the public is fascinated with aviation."

"It's not a living forever," he said. "There are no old stunt flyers. Either they come to their senses and stop while they're ahead, or they . . ." He paused, unable to put the words in an inoffensive way.

"Crash and burn." She conceded. "But if you know exactly what you're doing, and you're careful—"

He shook his head. "It's got nothing to do with being careful or being skilled. Surely you've heard of planes stalling, or wing tips caught on an unexpected piece of barbed wire, flipping them over. Remember Sam Goodwin? They said he was the best. He crashed on the airstrip practicing something he'd done hundreds of times before."

She was annoyed at his unwelcome frankness. "Nothing is certain. People have crashed on motorcycles."

"Why do you do it?" he asked, refusing to be sidetracked.

"Well, why not?" she responded sharply.

"I'll tell you two reasons," he said. "One, because the public may be fascinated with aviation, but they see flying as a freak show event. Their fascination is bound to wane one day. And two, because it's not worth risking your life to please a crowd that will never be satisfied." He carefully folded a tortilla over a spoonful of mashed beans.

Meredith watched Johnny fold the tortilla precisely, and suddenly she wondered what he was like as a child.

"They want more and more danger," he added when she hadn't spoken.

She pulled her attention back from the thought of Johnny as a serious child. "So, you give them the illusion of danger. I'm in control and what I do is very safe." She sat back, sipping her water.

"Are you really that blasé about it?" he asked.

She set her glass down and leaned forward, looking him straight in the eye. "Yes."

A cold chill jolted through him, and he thought of the risky dive she had performed to impress Meacham. Suddenly, he didn't want to be here with this bold girl who stupidly risked her life to please a fickle crowd. He questioned whether he'd heard God's voice about her. If the evening was to be salvaged, he thought, he should change the subject.

Meredith watched an emotion she couldn't identify flicker briefly in his eyes, then his dark eyebrows drew together, and he looked at her in an odd way. She felt the same way she did when her father told her to give up her silly notion of being an aviatrix. "You can call it blasé," she said, "but I call it confidence."

He took a deep breath in resignation. "Okay," he said, gesturing at her nearly empty plate. "Would you like dessert?"

She found his attitude vaguely disturbing. She wanted him to understand. "No, thanks," she said, reminding herself that she didn't care how he felt about her flying.

They talked about impersonal things: the weather on the west coast and the way people streamed to Los Angeles looking for paradise. He mentioned the arrival of a variety of preachers, easing into the subject in order to find out if Meredith was a believer.

She brightened and said, "Aimee Semple McPherson! I'd like to see her!" She was curious, both because the preacher was a woman, and because the brilliantly staged spectacles sounded much more dramatic than her father's somber meetings.

"Are you a believer?" Johnny was pleased that the subject came up so easily.

"Everyone believes in God," she said as the waiter appeared and asked them if there was anything else they'd like.

To avoid the subject Johnny had introduced, she tried to ask the waiter if he'd come directly from Mexico, but he excused himself, saying he was learning English and could not converse yet. He grinned and told the young *señorita* to come back soon, and he'd be *mas feliz* to talk with her.

They were quiet on the way home. The rain continued to drum on the roof as they sped through the night. Johnny felt frustrated, because the evening hadn't gone the way he'd hoped it would. Meredith held her hands in her lap, stroking the back of one with the thumb of the other while she watched the rain and wished it would go away. Tomorrow was crucial to her career. If she didn't fly for Meacham, she'd have to come up with an alternative plan.

five

When Meredith slipped into the apartment, Helen was seated on the couch, a magazine in her hand. "Tell me everything," she said, her features becoming animated.

Meredith shrugged, pulling the combs from her hair.

"Aw, Merry, have a heart! You go out with the most eligible bachelor in aviation and refuse to talk about it? Don't be cruel!"

"They're all eligible," said Meredith. "At least that's what they all say."

"That's the truth!" Helen slapped the magazine down. "At least tell me what you had for dinner."

Meredith paced in front of the window. "It was Mexican— oh, when is this rain going to stop?"

"It could stop any minute, or it could go on all night. It never rains more than two days at a time here."

"Meacham's just *got* to let me fly. I need the money and I need the publicity."

"You want to be famous?"

"Just to be known, have a good reputation, so when I open my flying school, people will want to come." She stared out into the night. "Stop it!"

"Are you telling the rain to quit?" Helen laughed. "While you're at it, tell the tide to come in."

With a long, exhausted sigh, Meredith turned her back to the dripping night. "You're right. I might as well wait and see what tomorrow brings."

Helen lifted her fist to the window and imitating Merry's voice, said to the dark clouds, "And tomorrow better be good!"

"That's right," Meredith agreed with a grin of amusement.

"If you won't talk about tonight, let's talk about tomorrow."
She went to the kitchen table and leaned over the papers laid
out on the gingham cloth. "Here's my new trick for this
weekend's show."

Helen had sketched out a transfer from one plane to another,
using a rope ladder.

Meredith grinned. "That trick is banned in some places."

"I know." She gave Meredith a conspiratorial wink. "What I
want to do is fly up with you, Joe will follow, and I'll climb
down the ladder onto the wing of my plane, where I'll do my
rain dance and the rest of my act."

Meredith was touched by Helen's wanting to help her ef-
forts. "I'd be glad to help you, of course, but . . ."

Helen waved away the rest of her words. "No buts about it.
I'll pay you one hundred dollars." She smiled at Merry's dazed
expression. "Of course, this will be extra for you, in addition
to your own act."

Meredith reached out and squeezed Helen's hand. "Thank
you. And tomorrow Meacham is going to bust his suspenders
when he sees my audition!" She looked upward at the tapping
of the rain on the roof. "<u>If</u> I get the chance, that is."

"*When* you get your chance," corrected Helen. "Tell me the
scariest thing you're going to do."

But Meredith was staring at the sketches. She pointed at one
of them. "Here!" She looked excitedly at Helen. "We'll put the
ladder on the top wing, I'll fly upside-down, and you climb
down onto your plane which Joe will maneuver directly beneath me. It's never been done before! The crowd will go crazy!"

Helen's eyes lit up. "I see it! I can do it!" She grabbed one of
the pencils and turned the page over to sketch on the other
side. She roughly drew the planes, one a mirror image of the
other, and a ladder hanging between them.

Meredith picked up a pencil and drew circles at the bottom
of the page. "These are the heads of the crowd. We'll fly low

over them so they can shiver and scream when you make the change."

Helen laughed. "You mean shiver with anticipation of something going wrong. That's why they really come out, you know. They're horrified when accidents happen, yet secretly that's what they come to see."

Her frank analysis of the crowd's avid hunger for more reckless, death-defying tricks was too uncomfortably close to what Johnny had said earlier. Meredith straightened her shoulders and placed her hands on her hips. "Well, they can shiver all they want, but we won't give them an accident."

Helen straightened the papers and laid the pencils beside them. "Of course not. Let's practice early tomorrow and be ready to show Meacham." She laughed at Meredith's uncertain glance upward. "Hey, I can undo this with an unrain dance!" She skipped into the living room and spun around near the door.

"My plane's at Johnny's hangar," said Meredith.

"Really!"

Meredith shook her head, suppressing a grin. "It's just business."

"Sure." Helen's black eyes flashed with mischief. "I'll take you to his place to pick up your plane." She opened the door, and cool air flooded the room. "I'd better use Johnny's phone to call Joe and let him know we're working early tomorrow."

The next morning Meredith slapped the clock before it started to ring. She crawled up, placing her knees on her pillow, stretched up to the window over the nightstand between the twin beds, and peeked out behind the shade. The sky was gray but with blue patches. On the ground, a drop splashed into a puddle. Soon another fell. But those blue patches cheered her. *It's quitting!* she thought, with joy.

She ran water in the bath, and while she was making coffee, Helen entered the kitchen, tying the belt of her red and white silk wrapper.

Meredith set two cups on the counter. "I'll take a quick bath, have my coffee, and we can be out of here by six-thirty."

"I hope Joe got the message I left with his landlady." Helen went into the living room, and pulled back the curtain, and looked out toward the ocean.

Meredith's joy was not to be dampened. "I can feel it! This is going to be a wonderful day! I just know it!"

She hurried through her bath, put on her jumpsuit, and looked over the sketches once more while Helen combed her hair and gathered her things. A soft knock at the door startled her.

She opened it to find Johnny standing on the steps. "Yes?" she asked. Helen came out, carrying a leather helmet.

Johnny's glance slid from Meredith to Helen, and he said, "Joe just called. He can't meet you at Meacham's, because his brother rode his motorcycle home last night and won't have it back until nine o'clock. He wants to know why you're going up so early."

"We have a lot of practicing to do before Meacham shows up at noon," said Helen, frowning at this development. "Joe lives in Pasadena. Shall I pick him up first, or take you to your plane first?" she asked Meredith, folding the helmet into a large leather bag.

Johnny spoke up. "I'm leaving now, so I'll take Meredith with me, and you can get Joe. That'll save time."

Meredith started to protest, but any other way would use up precious time, so she thanked Johnny, and quickly looked away, pretending to be looking for something important.

Over her shoulder she said to Helen, "See you at the field," and followed Johnny out onto the damp sidewalk. The air smelled clean, of damp grass mingled with the salty smell of the ocean. A drop of rain fell on her arm as she walked beside him.

At his apartment he stepped aside, holding the door open

for her. "Come in out of the rain for a minute while I get a couple things." Being in his apartment seemed very intimate, and Merry had the urge to run back outside and stand on the porch. But she stayed while he disappeared through a doorway.

The room was spartan, almost bare. The only two pieces of furniture were a sofa and chair, and against one wall a shelf of books stood beside a tilted drawing board covered with neat piles of papers.

Meredith was drawn to a large painting of an airplane flying over a lovely farmland scene, which filled the wall over the sofa. She leaned forward, her knees pressing into the cushions, examining the picture, when Johnny startled her by coming into the room. She fell forward, grabbing the back of the sofa for support.

He reached out to steady her, holding her arms longer than necessary, unable to let go.

She looked over her shoulder up into his face for a moment, noticing that same odd faraway look she'd seen before. She glanced down at his hands on her arms, and he released her.

"My mother painted this," he said.

"It's lovely." She rubbed the warm spot on her arm where he'd touched her, took a deep breath, and said, "Ready?"

Johnny's eyes lingered on her a moment, remembering when she'd first introduced herself. She was looking at him, and he realized she'd asked him something. "I'm ready," he said.

Driving south beside the coast, he tried to imagine a life with Meredith. He didn't know her very well, but what he did know of her he found attractive, except for her insistence on flying through the skies like a maniac. How would she react if he asked her to marry him and stop flying? Probably laugh and run so fast his head would swim.

"In New York I got used to seeing the sun rise over the ocean," she said, looking out at the gray waves, hoping the wind would shift and blow the dark clouds away from the land. "Here, that's where it sets."

"Tell me about New York," he said, turning away from the coastline. He stopped for more of those fragrant cinnamon rolls and coffee, and talking lightly, they reached the hangar before seven o'clock.

Johnny pulled the wide doors open. "I'm flying a businessman to San Diego this morning." He looked up at the windsock. "I'll have a tailwind all the way."

Together they examined the extension she'd worked so hard on. "It's dry!" he exclaimed, smiling with satisfaction. "And looks new, as if it came from Curtiss's factory!" He crossed his arms and leaned against the workbench. "If you get tired of risking life and limb, you've got a job here as a mechanic."

"I'm risking life and limb, as you call it, as a step toward my goal of teaching others to fly," she replied, bristling with indignation. She was getting tired of hearing about the dangers of stunt flying.

"Of course," he said, silently berating himself for saying the wrong thing again.

six

The rain had let up, and the skies were mostly blue with patches of clouds, instead of the other way round as they had been yesterday. Meredith veered out over the shoreline, close to the foaming waves as they broke over the beach. She taxied down Meacham's grass runway to a stop beside Helen's plane and cut the engine.

The air smelled wet and fresh in the quiet morning. She took off her goggles, loosened her helmet straps, and shook out her hair. Stretching her arms straight up, she broke into a big grin. "Today's the day! The first step toward my *own* business!" She leaned her head back against the leather cockpit edge and closed her eyes, rehearsing the trick she and Helen were going to show Meacham this afternoon.

Then she imagined herself going through her own routine. She was in the midst of flying upside-down between the bleachers when she heard the car, and she ran to meet Helen and Joe.

First they went up and simply flew the formation, with Joe staying directly under Meredith as she flew in inverted position for the time Helen would need to make the change; then Joe dipped slightly and Meredith peeled off, righting her plane.

They landed and fastened the rope to Birdie's top wing. "I'll get out and climb between the wings, holding the wires just before you turn upside-down," said Helen. "Then I'll climb down to our right wing. When I let go of the ladder, Joe, wait a minute for me to grab the ring."

"Before we actually do this trick," Meredith said, "let's go up one more time, and you climb out onto the wing, so I can get the feel of the weight and how much compensation I'll need to keep stable."

"Good idea," said Helen. "Joe, watch us, and when we buzz you, come on up." She pulled both rings on her plane's top wings, checked the struts and wires, and when she was satisfied everything was secure, she checked the rope on Meredith's plane and got into the front cockpit.

Meredith circled out over the beach, flew low over the field, and Helen climbed out onto the wing. With the wind fiercely whipping her, she gripped the wires while Meredith slowly inverted her position, and got the feel of the extra weight on the wing. She righted herself, came back over the field, and did it again.

Helen slid into the front cockpit, grinning at Meredith with her thumb up. Meredith buzzed the field, and Joe took off.

The trick went perfectly, and Meredith waved good-bye to them as they worked on other stunts. She flew to an open area and did some practicing, but the wind became strong enough to cause her to retreat back to the Venice field. The earlier clouds which had seemed harmless now had multiplied and turned dark on the bottom. She taxied up beside Helen's plane.

"I don't know about this weather," said Joe. "Looks like more rain. Maybe we should put the plane inside."

"Joe!" warned Meredith. "Don't even say it."

"Say what?"

She looked up at the clouds, then gave him a significant look. "It's going to be a *clear* afternoon."

Helen eyed the clouds, looked at Joe, and said, "It's very important that Merry audition for Meacham."

"Right!" said Meredith. "What time is it?"

Joe checked his watch and said, "Eleven o'clock."

Meredith flattened her palms against her legs. "Let's go." This was the day she'd been working toward all week, and she was ready.

"Let's get a sandwich first," said Joe. "We'll be back long

before Meacham arrives."

Meredith hesitated. "What if he's early?"

Helen patted her shoulder. "Gotta feed my flyer. Come on. We have plenty of time."

Meredith was so nervous she could hardly eat. In spite of willing the skies to be clear and refusing to even mention the word, rain began falling softly onto the outside table where they were eating.

They returned to Meacham's field. Aviators, chutists, and wing walkers were inside the hangar out of the rain. Their colorful planes sat on the field like a child's scattered toys.

Kate LaFore and two of the mock Air Force flyers arrived in a yellow phaeton with the top down, ignoring the rain. They wove through the cars parked near the gate and stopped beneath the bleacher overhang. A party atmosphere surrounded them as they lit up cigarettes and laughed at something one of them said.

Helen rolled her eyes. "Heap big squaw," she said.

Meredith covered a smile with her hand.

"Come on, Merry," said Helen. "Let's go inside."

"No! It's stopping any minute now!" Meredith scowled at the sky, as if it were a naughty child, raining just to annoy her. If she stayed outside, stubbornly refusing to acknowledge the drops falling on her head, the clouds just might give up and let her have her way.

"You need stronger medicine than a wish and a fierce look." When Meredith refused to budge, Helen laughed. "Come on, Joe." They ran inside the hangar.

Meredith stood in the gathering rain, feeling foolish and frustrated. Kate and her men were shrieking with laughter; the murmur of voices from the hangar floated out to her, and she stood near her plane, feeling lonely.

She wondered if Johnny's trip to San Diego had gone well, how far away he was, and if the sky was raining there. He'd looked at her in such an odd way in his apartment this morning and had been strangely silent in the car on the way to his hangar. She was trying to remember that faraway look he had in his eyes, trying to figure out what it meant, when Meacham arrived.

He had the barker with him. Kate and her entourage leaped from their car, and joined him, running into the hangar. Meredith walked through the sodden grass, not caring that her boots were getting wet.

She entered a different door than the one Meacham had gone through, and found herself behind the parachutists. Meacham had a roll of handbills under his arm, and he raised the other to quiet the group. Meredith flicked moisture from her curls and watched him carefully.

"I have it on good authority that this rain will pass by midnight tonight." The group greeted that announcement with joy.

Meredith thought the rain would have done better to stop right now. She needed to convince Meacham that he needed her in his circus.

He unfurled the handbill, titled "MEACHAM'S WILD WEST FLYING CIRCUS" with drawings of planes, parachutes, and wingwalkers around the edges. In smaller letters was written, "Death Defying Aerial Antics, including a Dive of Death." He passed a few handbills through the group.

Beside Kate's name was a drawing of her on a wing, looking as though she were dancing in a ballroom. Beneath were smaller words, calling her America's supreme ballerina of the air. Helen's name was prominent, above the name of a "Master Aviator" and his picture. Time, place, and 25-cent admission charge was the bottom line.

He raised his hand again to quiet them. "You're wondering about the Dive of Death." Meredith's heart beat faster. He was going to let her do the dive! "Basically, what it amounts to," he continued, "is that Bob Simms, who we'll call Rowdy Bob,

will hang by his knees from a plane and drop into a haystack."
Meredith bit her lip in disappointment as Meacham grinned at
the barker. "And Sam, I want you to emphasize that he has no
parachute!" Sam's eyes lit up at the thought. "Make the crowd
think he might not make it."

Sam grinned, and Meacham nodded in satisfaction. He paced
as he talked. "I won't ask you to perform for me today, as I
know you all, and trust you to put on a good show. So each one
tell me what you've planned for the weekend." He gestured to
Kate. "You're first."

Meredith's heart plummeted. He'd forgotten about her, and
she wouldn't even have a chance to fly for him. Her throat
ached as each flyer described tricks bolder and crazier than the
last. When Helen mentioned her plane change, he didn't question who'd be working the other plane.

He'd gone around the room and finally spotted her in the
back. "Oh, yes. Miss . . . I forgot your name, honey," he said.

Meredith felt all eyes on her, and a hot flush crept into her
cheeks. She narrowed her eyes and took a deep breath to steady
herself. "Bailey," she answered. "Meredith Bailey." He was
moving toward her, and the jumpers in front of her moved
aside.

"Well, Miss Bailey," he said, looking down and scratching
an eyebrow, "I'm sorry, but you'll have to wait until next week.
I want to see your work before I put your name on the handbill."

After an instant of stunned silence, Meredith recovered, held
her head high, and stepped forward. Looking up into his surprised face, she said, "I've worked hard. My stunts are so spectacular, you need them this week."

His mouth dropped open, and he looked at her in surprise.
"I'm impressed by your enthusiasm and the fire in your eyes,"
he said, shaking his head. "But I have my rules."

She started to talk, but he stopped her. "I'll tell you what, though. Bring that purple bird cage and you can take riders up after the show." He smiled at her as though he'd offered her ownership of the circus. Obviously pleased with himself, he turned and addressed the group. "That's it! Meeting adjourned."

The group broke into conversation, and the parachutists gathered around Mr. Meacham.

Helen put her arm around Meredith's shoulder. "Don't feel bad. It's a start."

"It's not enough! I *need* to fly!" She suddenly felt selfish. "I'm sorry. It's not your fault. You've given me the chance to at least get up there during the show." She frowned. "Maybe when I peel off after you make the transfer—no, I can't detract from your act." She twisted a curl on the left side of her neck, thinking. At least she'd be in the air, but she had to find a way to get Meacham's attention while she was there, without risking making him angry.

&

After Johnny delivered his businessman to San Diego, he checked in at the small airfield office. A map of the area filled one wall, with elevations, airfields, and distances marked. Beside the map were tacked ads and notes. He found a cup on the table beneath the notes, poured himself some coffee, and dropped a nickel in the jar.

Then he reached into the row of wooden boxes containing notes and messages. There were two envelopes and one small package to deliver back to Los Angeles.

A large, bald man named Adam Shelton sat at the paperstrewn desk near the window on the opposite wall. "Westmore! You just missed a customer. He needed to get to Tijuana immediately."

Johnny took a sip of coffee, relieved that he wouldn't have to refuse a passenger probably involved in rum-running.

Shelton pushed aside a layer of papers and notes, and finally pulled a bank draft from beneath a Zeppelin paperweight. He handed Johnny the payment for delivering letters and packages.

Since there were no sightseeing passengers waiting, Johnny took the trolley into town and went to the local radio station. He arranged for a spot advertising Westmore Airline's scheduled trip daily to Los Angeles, ninety minutes for only $14.50 for passengers, and a minimal amount for messages and packages. If he could get enough business, he'd keep an airplane based in San Diego and hire someone to fly daily round trips.

He visited the post office to see if they had an answer yet to his offer to deliver mail to any California city. The person he needed to speak with was in an all-day meeting, so he ate a late lunch and went back to the airfield.

The flying school plane taxied down the runway and took off. He thought of Meredith and her purple Jenny, and his mouth curved into a thoughtful smile. If he built another hangar and let her start her school on his airfield, would she do it?

Even if she did, why would he do such a thing, anyway? To have her near? He stood outside the office, thinking for a long time. Daredevils come and go, Meacham's show could suddenly move on to a new area, another circus might offer her more money, or she could find a place for her school hundreds of miles away.

He believed the small Voice he'd heard in church last week, and he knew he had to do something to keep her in Los Angeles. What would she'd do if he came right out and told her she was going to be his wife some day? Probably think he was screwy and tell him so. Resolving to start this very evening to win her over, his heart swelled with the certainty that he was doing the right thing.

He leaped the three steps into the office and checked with Shelton to see if there were any sightseers wanting a fifteen-minute coast excursion.

seven

Johnny delivered his passenger to the Los Angeles Terminal at Ninety-ninth and Western, then hopped over to his field, got on his motorcycle, delivered the packages, and finally drove his car home through the dark. He grinned at the light in Helen's apartment, relishing the thought of seeing Meredith.

He cleaned up and changed clothes, putting on plain gray pants, a white shirt, and a casual grey knitted vest. He wanted to avoid looking like he was going courting (even if that was the case).

He knocked on Helen's door, trying to ignore the rumbling of his stomach. Lunch had been a long time ago. No matter. Maybe Meredith would accompany him for another dinner. She could eat dessert, and . . .

Helen opened the door, a folded newspaper in her hand. "Johnny! Come on in." Then she thrust the paper at his chest. "The password is a seven-letter word for hired gunman."

Johnny narrowed his eyes, thinking for a second. "Torpedo."

She moved aside to let him enter, counting the spaces. "T-O-R-P-E-D-O. Fits!" She pursed her lips. "But that's a slang word. No fair!"

Johnny looked quickly aside for Meredith, then chuckled. "Don't tell me the crossword craze has gotten you!"

"Oh, I work one once in a while," she said nonchalantly. "Have a seat." She gestured to the sofa.

He eyed it as if considering staying but said, "How did Miss Bailey's audition go?"

Helen dropped down on the sofa, put the paper on the table beside it, and slowly shook her head with a troubled frown.

"What happened?"

Her eyes reflected sympathy as she looked up at him. "The rain didn't let up, and she didn't get to fly for him."

He shoved his hands in his pockets and sighed heavily. "Where is she?"

Helen nodded toward the door. "Gone walking on the beach."

"Thanks." He stepped toward the door. He motioned Helen to stay seated. "I'll talk to her."

She smiled. "Thank *you*, Johnny."

He closed the door quietly and loped down the steps. As he crossed the beach esplanade, sand poured into his shoes, so he took them off and stuffed his socks inside them.

He stood for a moment looking both ways. To his right a few couples strolled along the esplanade, and he could just make out the sound of music floating out from a restaurant where light spilled out onto the beach. To his left a lone man and his dog walked near the breakers, and the light of a boat bobbed in the dark water a few hundred feet out. He jogged in that direction, scanning the darkness for Meredith's small form.

He almost missed her, but at last he found her sitting up against a large piece of driftwood, staring out at the sea.

He stood before her, swinging his shoes by his fingers. "A penny for your thoughts."

She smiled weakly up at him. "They're really not worth that much."

"Not even a penny?" He sat beside her.

She sighed. "How'd you find me?"

"Just lucky," he said. "Helen told me you didn't get to fly for Meacham today."

She looked up at the traitorous sky. "No."

He dug his heel into the sand. She was so pretty in the soft light, lovelier and more feminine than any woman he'd ever known. "So you could help Curley and me sell rides."

She studied his lean, dark face, thinking that no one should be allowed to have eyes that see right into your heart. She touched her fingertips to her forehead. "Thanks, Captain, but Meacham *did* say I could take up passengers after the show."

He rewarded her with a large smile. "Well, then. That's a start!"

She gazed out over the ocean, feeling a strange sensation of comfort in his words. "I'm also doing a stunt with Helen and Joe, but I'm thinking of ways to get Meacham's attention while I'm up, without detracting from her."

Just then his stomach growled, and she quickly looked at him. He shrugged one shoulder. "Early lunch and no supper." His eyes pleaded with her. "Care to join me and tell me your ideas?" She opened her mouth, but he held up his hand. "It's okay if you've already eaten. You can watch me or have a dessert or something."

She thought of Kate LaFore and her flirtatious male friends. *If Kate can keep them at arm's length, I can, too,* thought Meredith. Her mouth quirked with humor. "Yes, I'll join you. I ate an apple, but I'm hungry again. And yes, I'd tell you my ideas if I thought any of them would actually work."

He held his hand down to her. "Shall we go then?" She reached up to him and he pulled her to a standing position. "Smart girl. You're wearing boots."

"But I can't wear them into a restaurant. I'll have to change clothes," she said. "It'll take a few minutes."

He held his hand to his stomach and groaned. "I can't wait another minute!"

She made a sad face as they slogged through the sand. "Poor baby."

"I know a place where we can get a good dinner, and we'll drive into the hills to eat it."

"A moonlight picnic!" Meredith started to run ahead of him. In spite of her resolve to be cautious, she felt reckless and in need of some excitement. Johnny overtook her, and they hopped into his car. He shook the sand from his socks and shoes and put them on, and they sped away.

He pulled into the parking lot of a diner. "Reach behind you," he said. "On the floor is a basket."

Meredith retrieved the basket, and they took it inside. He bought roast beef sandwiches, which the waitress put into a paper sack, potatoes and gravy spooned into a jar, a can of pears, two bottles of root beer, and a handful of mints.

They packed the dinner into the basket, and he grasped her hand as they went out the door. Her slim fingers were almost lost in his larger ones.

She laughed and pulled her hand away from his. "Do you always carry an empty basket with clean jars and silverware just in case you get hungry?"

He helped her into her seat, saying, "My mother sends me a square meal from time to time." He shut her door and went around to his, then put the basket between them. "I think it's to remind me that I haven't been over to see her for a while," he added with a spark of amusement in his eyes.

As they made their way up the new Mulhullond Drive, Meredith was unable to keep herself from taking surreptitious peeks at him, admiring what she saw. His handsome face, dark against the moonlight, and his blue eyes with their secrets pleased her. Her hand still felt warm from being in his, she thought dreamily, before catching herself. She looked the other way, frowning at her silly fantasies, willing her wayward imagination back into line.

"This is as far as I can go," he said, and pulled off into a clearing overlooking the city. "The smell of that roast beef is driving me crazy."

Meredith looked out over the lights below as he opened the basket. "It's beautiful," she breathed. "And so quiet up here."

He handed her a sandwich and looked out over the view. "L.A. is booming. People come in droves from all over the world. I read in the paper last week that Los Angeles is five times larger today than it was in 1900." He pulled a dish from the basket and handed it to her.

"What brings them?"

"Mostly the weather. There's oil to drill, movies to make, souls to save, land deals to close, more building, more jobs, more everything!"

He unscrewed the potatoes and gravy and spooned half of it onto her plate. "I'll use the spoon, and you can have the fork. We'll have to fight over the knife." He opened the can of pears and gave her half, then handed her a root beer.

He got very still for a minute, and she waited to see what he'd do next. He bowed his head. "Thank You, God, for this food and for the fellowship. Amen," he said quietly.

Meredith closed her eyes for the brief prayer, and when he was through, she quietly put the root beer on the floor beside her feet, looking down to hide her thoughts, surprised again by this unpredictable man. She unwrapped the sandwich from the plate balanced on her lap. She'd never met an aviator who claimed to believe in God.

Quickly changing the subject, she said, "In the midwest people have dreams of coming to California, sitting in the sun, and eating oranges."

He laughed. "Some do! They scrape up whatever they can, come here, and put a down payment on a home."

"Well," she said, sipping her root beer, "the more who come, the better for the Circus."

They talked of the Circus while they ate, but they could not come up with a stunt Meredith could do without alienating Meacham.

They finished their meal, got out of the car, and munched on the mints while leaning against the fender in the cool night air. "Meredith! Look up," Johnny said, pointing. "There's the Big Dipper and the North Star."

"Oh!" she said. "They're so bright." She looked down at the city lights. "Those down there are pale imitations."

"But with the know-how that brought us from fire to electric lights, we may someday even figure how to fly right up to one of those stars."

She tried to suppress a giggle. "Those are suns! You'd burn up if you got near one. By the way, you can call me Merry."

"Thanks, Merry. But they're not all suns. There must be somewhere up there we can land, once we figure out how to get there."

He looked up, with that faraway, dreamy look in his eyes again. She looked up too and tried to imagine what it would be like to fly right off the earth that far. "Nobody would live long enough to travel that far."

He sighed. "There are lots of problems to overcome." His eyes beckoned with mystery. "Someday someone will find a way."

She forced herself to look away. "Well, for now, I need to find a way to fly right here at Meacham's field."

"We've thought of just about everything, short of flying in behind the squadron."

She laughed, thinking of her purple Jenny merrily following a squadron of fierce fighters.

"Where did you grow up?" asked Johnny.

"Oh, in the East," she said vaguely. She didn't want to talk about her life in England as the daughter of a traveling preacher. She got quiet, thinking of her father, wondering how he was doing and reminding herself it was time for her monthly letter to him.

He was silent in the aftermath of her vague answer. She clearly didn't want to talk about herself, and Johnny wondered why. He looked down at the top of her head, enjoying being with her.

She pushed away from the car. "Thanks for the dinner. It's

getting late, and we should start back."

He was reluctant to leave but glad for the good time they had had together. She was quiet as they started down the hill.

As they neared the apartments, he got an idea. "You said Meacham will let you take riders up?"

"Yes," she said. "He acted like he was handing me a starring role with Rudolf Valentino."

"Well, in a way you can be the star of the passenger flights."

"What do you mean?"

"What if you offer a simple trick with your ride, like a slow roll?"

She sat straight up and looked at him, wide-eyed. "That would work! None of the other aviators offer a trick too!"

"And none of them has a purple plane," he added. He turned the car onto their street. "Why is she painted purple, anyway?"

"I was going to paint her blue, and call her the Bluebird of Happiness," said Merry, "but I realized the color blue wouldn't contrast with the sky and wouldn't be easily seen. I found the purple paint at a good price and called her Birdie."

"You painted the plane yourself?" he asked, looking at her in amazement.

"Of course. She didn't come all assembled and painted in the crate."

"You assembled it, too?"

"Of course. I had some help lifting the heavy parts, but I did all the work to make her ready to fly. Buying the tools was the hardest part."

He parked beside his apartment and continued to stare at her, imagining her assembling the plane, stretching fabric over the wood, painting on the dope, layer upon layer. He'd never heard of a woman with that much determination.

She began to feel uncomfortable under his scrutiny. She reached for the door handle. "Well, thanks for the dinner and the ride."

He quickly got out and came around to open her door. "My pleasure. Let's do it again soon."

Her delight at the idea of being alone with him again worried her. He guided her to her doorstep and stood awkwardly for a moment, as if he wanted to say something more. Instead, he reached out and gently touched a loose golden corkscrew of hair beside her cheek. "Good night, Merry," he said.

"Good night," she said in a voice that seemed to come from a long way off and slipped inside. She leaned against the door frame and put her fingers on the spot where he'd brushed her cheek.

Helen strolled into the room, startling her. Meredith snatched her hand from her cheek and moved away from the door.

Helen's long, black hair hung over one shoulder as she braided it. "You were on the beach for a long time." She looked down as she finished her braid. "Did Johnny find you?"

"He did." Meredith walked into the kitchen and got the bottle of milk from the icebox.

Helen followed her. "And?"

Meredith poured milk into a glass and leaned casually against the counter. "We talked, and he gave me an idea for tomorrow's show." She sipped the cool milk.

Helen waited for more, her mouth pursed and eyes wide.

"I'm going to take the riders on an easy slow roll."

Helen's face beamed. "Why didn't *we* think of that?" She narrowed her eyes. "It's perfect, it's simple, and it won't make the rider sick—the slow roll is just enough for a thrill, but not enough to scare them to death."

Merry drank more of the milk and felt herself relaxing. She smiled. "Just what I thought."

Helen reached for a glass and poured some milk for herself. "That Johnny Westmore! A flapper would say 'he's the bee's knees.'"

Meredith grinned. "Bee's knees. Visualize them," she said.

"For instance, I came here from the 'Bible Belt.' Imagine a belt made of Bibles!"

"Speak easy! A talking room that won't shut up?" Helen laughed. "Meacham, the big cheese!"

They poked fun at modern slang for a while longer, giggling.

Rinsing her glass, Merry said, "Let's go out tomorrow morning early, and practice one more time, all right?"

"Good idea. But now, let's get to bed."

When the lights were off, Helen murmured, "Good night, Merry. I'm glad you're here."

"Good night. Me too," said Merry. She stared into the darkness, remembering when she flew into Los Angeles, just a week ago. The first person she saw was Johnny; she had thought he was Meacham.

Joining the Air Circus was just what she needed to boost her depleting cash supply. Or at least she thought it was. An odd restlessness and yearning for something she couldn't name stirred inside her. She gently touched her cheek where his fingers had brushed it. He'd said good night in the same soft voice as he'd said grace over their picnic.

No matter how she tried to stick strictly to the events, it was his compelling, magnetic eyes she remembered the most. She rolled over onto her stomach, telling herself she had no time for a man. Maybe sometime, but not now. Right now her career was the most important thing in her life.

Forcing her mind to relive each step of Helen's stunt, planning how she'd fasten straps to the seat so her riders wouldn't fall out, she kept thoughts of Johnny away. But she curled her fingers, remembering the feel of his hand grasping hers as they ran to the car with their basket dinner, and she drifted to sleep with a smile.

eight

Meredith and Helen were at the field by seven-thirty. Helen pointed out that the rain clouds were gone, leaving a few harmless little wisps of white, and the winds were light. Meredith grudgingly agreed the weather was good, still feeling betrayed by yesterday's rain.

Helen insisted on putting gas into Meredith's plane, saying she was only being fair, since the practice runs were mostly for herself. Meredith fastened straps to the wicker seat in the front cockpit, and they went up. Helen tested the straps during one roll, to be sure a passenger would stay put, then got out and stood on the wing while Merry maneuvered to inverted flight. By the time they taxied down the field, Joe had arrived, and they went up again, doing the stunt. Then Helen and Joe worked their routines while Merry climbed, looped, and rolled to keep in practice for the day when she'd have her part in the show.

Johnny arrived at his hangar early, and he and Ernie put the finishing touches on the four-passenger enclosed cabin they built on the modified large Standard. They rolled it out onto the grass. Ernie cranked the prop, and Johnny and Curley took it up.

When they landed, Curly's eyes were as big as silver dollars. "Let's take it to the Circus! Think of the bucks we'll make hauling four at a time!"

"My idea, exactly," said Johnny, walking under the wing and inspecting the work. "But not only for the money, but because this will demonstrate that planes are not a passing fad for circus clowns to amuse a fickle mob."

"Yeah! And those cake-eaters will love it!"

Johnny worked the rudder and said, "Where do you get that slang? And what is a cake-eater anyway?"

"I get around," said Curly as he wiped a smudge of oil from the tail skid. "Cake-eater, a ladies' man, a sheik."

Johnny raised his left eyebrow a fraction. "You know, soon you'll be flying one of these things, instead of just working on them. It'll give you something else to think about besides cake-eaters and flappers."

"I'm ready to fly now!"

Johnny put a hand on his shoulder. "Remember I said when you're sixteen I'll start giving you lessons."

Curly rolled his eyes. "Four more months," he groaned.

"You've worked hard getting the Standard ready. I'm delivering packages to San Diego. Want to come along?"

Curly rubbed his palms together as they walked into the hangar. "Yeah!" He scrunched his face in a grimace. "But what if you get a passenger back to Los Angeles?"

Johnny slid the hangar door open in front of his DeHaviland. "Then I'll just have to leave you there," he said over his shoulder. Curly grinned, knowing Johnny better than that. They loaded the packages and took off.

Listening to the steady roar of the engines, looking down as he followed the road south, Johnny thought of Meredith's desire to open a flying school. Young boys like Curley would flock to learn from her. It was a worthy ambition, but there must be a better way than risking her life to get there. She could use her secretarial skills—but he knew that doing what you love and getting paid for it was the best motivator in the world.

❧

Meredith followed Joe and Helen to Meacham's field, arriving an hour before the first show. At least fifty cars were already parked in the lots behind both bleachers, and people were claiming the best seats. Lines were beginning to form in front of the food booths.

She and Helen carried their flying costumes into the hangar. In an area screened off for privacy, they hung them on pegs. "I'm going to attach a target on one wing and shoot an arrow at it," said Helen, taking off her jacket.

"With all that wind, you'll be lucky if you hit the target at all," said Merry, sitting on the stool to remove her shoes.

"I've got it all figured out."

A woman parachute jumper slipped in behind the screen and dropped her armload of clothes, boots, and jacket next to Helen. "Another day, another dollar," she said, pulling up her blue wool jumpsuit. She grumbled about the wind and the weather, left her clothes in a pile, and wished them luck as she left.

Merry's mind was whirling with her own thoughts. "I need a sign and a way to put it up."

"It all depends on where Meacham puts you. You can attach it to mine if you're near me."

"I'd better find him so I can begin working on it."

Meacham put her last in line, next to Johnny's booth. When she'd finished her hastily made sign, she rolled it up, took two boards, and headed toward her assigned position. She squared her shoulders and narrowed her eyes, envisioning a sign that said "Bailey's Flying School."

Sam's voice barked out promises of unimaginable thrills as he walked up and down in front of the almost filled bleachers. People leaned out over the rails to catch a glimpse of an aviator or parachutist. Near the end of the runway Jorge and a mechanic had opened the doors of the last hangar, and the nose of Kate LaFore's plane gleamed in the slanted sunshine. Johnny's plane was tied down outside beside Meredith's.

She avoided even a glance in the direction of Johnny's booth. She stood in the mashed grass beside it, wondering how she'd get the two poles into the ground. Curley cleared his throat and said, "Can I help?"

As she looked at his red, curly hair and large freckles, she couldn't help but return his grin as he twisted his cap in his hands.

"Thank you," she said, glancing past him, seeing that Johnny was nowhere near. Together they mounted her sign. He hovered close to her, telling her about his desire to fly and that Johnny was going to teach him, and she thought how easily a boy could find an instructor.

She wondered where Johnny was but wouldn't ask. As though reading her thoughts, Curley nodded toward the last hangar and said, "Johnny's over there, helping Miss LaFore's mechanic. Ernie brings the truck with spare parts, and Johnny's helping find the right one. These planes can be tricky at times—you know? Stalling at the wrong time, oil burning. One time I saw—"

A military trumpet signalled the beginning of the show, and the crowd cheered as the airborne armada buzzed the field, with the red and gold Meacham's Wild West Flying Circus sign fluttering behind the last plane. Meredith and Curly stood beside the hangars, watching the fantastic stunts and gasping with the crowd when it looked as though one of the parachutes wouldn't open in time.

She and Helen performed the plane-to-plane transfer flawlessly. Meredith landed quickly and carefully, so as not to distract the crowd delighting in Helen's Indian stunts.

The last act, the Dive of Death that ended with the daredevil falling into the haystack and the local ambulance careening down the runway, had the crowd in a panic. No one could contain them as they poured out of the bleachers, only to see the ambulance drive away with the supposedly injured man inside. They were keyed up and eager to get a closer look at one of these flying machines, even take a ride in one themselves.

The more cautious went up in Johnny's plane, and the bolder ones went up with Meredith. She tried to suppress her smiles at the brave young men impressing their girlfriends, while skeptical about a woman at the controls. One man insisted he didn't need to be strapped in; he didn't think she'd do anything that could scare him. But Meredith firmly buckled the straps anyway. She took him through two rolls, and when they landed he was speechless and suspiciously pale.

Word spread that her ride was a rip-roaring spin, and when Sam came through with his megaphone, shouting that the next show was due to start in half an hour and the crowd would have to leave, there were many disappointed would-be passengers. One hung back, rudely jostling closer to Meredith so he could ask her to see him after the show. She laughed and told him she wasn't interested.

He stepped nearer and eyed her.

She tried to keep her smile and looked the man straight in his eyes. In a friendly way, she said, "Sorry, I don't date men I don't know."

"You could get to know me, if you'll see me afterward." He put his hand on her upper arm.

She detected the faint smell of liquor, but she didn't flinch. "I told you—"

"Get your hands off the lady."

Meredith hadn't seen him coming, and before she could react, Johnny's large body was wedged between her and the man.

"What's it to you?" asked the man with a sneer. Meredith stepped around to Johnny's side. Curley was standing near.

"The lady said no, pal. So you'd better leave."

"I wasn't talking to you." The man moved closer to Meredith, and Johnny intervened again.

She bristled, watching them. Though they were arguing about her, they were ignoring her. "Excuse me," she said, trying to step in front of Johnny. "I can take care of this."

He shifted his weight slightly but didn't move. "I don't think his intentions are honorable."

"I can take care of it," she repeated.

The man grinned triumphantly at Johnny, but his smile faded when he looked at Merry.

She advanced toward him and thrust her finger at his chest. "I told you I don't date men I don't know." She poked at his chest again. "And I won't see you afterward." She poked again. "And, if I ever want to get to know you, I'll write it on a banner and fly it behind my plane." She put her hands on her hips. "But don't strain your neck looking up for the message."

The man shrugged his shoulders. "I may carry a torch to my grave because of you," he said as he walked away.

Behind her, Johnny could almost see the energy radiating from her as she stood, resolutely watching the man depart. Then she turned and hit him full force with the fire in her eyes. She stared at him as he studied her thoughtfully.

Johnny searched the green eyes that flashed with anger. He saw a familiar light and felt it pass between them, and he was pleased. He tried to look deeper, needing to know more about her.

"You were keen!" Curley's voice shattered the intense awareness they shared.

Merry pulled her gaze away from Johnny and blinked at Curley's bright smile. Something significant had happened during her visual interchange with Johnny. Quickly, she banished the thought.

Through the next show, Johnny adjusted an aileron, meditating on his reaction when he thought the man was getting too close to Meredith. He'd ruthlessly protect his family and loved ones. That thought barely crossed his mind before the thought followed that he couldn't protect her as long as she continued flitting around the sky in an unreliable, cranky Jenny.

After the show and rides, Helen introduced her brother and

his wife, who'd come to see her perform. She invited Meredith, Johnny, and Curley to join them to celebrate, but they declined, feeling the gathering was a family affair. Johnny offered to take Meredith home.

"I'm starved. Let's eat," said Curley, as they tied their planes down for the night.

Meredith performed Birdie's check over to be sure all the bolts were tight, the wires taut, and there were no oil spots. She longed to go straight to the apartment and be alone to think. So much had happened. She actually flew in the circus! She tightened a bolt holding the wire pulley, thinking about how much money she'd made. There was the hundred dollars promised by Helen, and after the two shows today she'd flown twenty-five people. She'd get part of the seven dollars per ride and Meacham would get part, but possibly she'd get as much as five dollars. At Sunday's meeting she'd actually receive money!

Curley put his face in front of her. "Miss Bailey!"

"Oh!" Merry's thoughts came back to the present. "What?" She blinked, to find them both looking at her.

Johnny smiled. "It seems you were somewhere up in the clouds. How about coming down to earth and joining us mortals for a meal?"

"Oh, no. I have too much to do!"

"You have to eat." He said, buttoning his jacket.

"Come on!" Curley stood on one foot, then the other, unable to keep still.

"There's food in our icebox, and I really have a lot to do," she said firmly.

They accepted this and drove to the apartment, each encouraged over their successes. Johnny felt he'd advanced the respectability of flying, Meredith was pleased to have taken another step toward her flying school, and Curley was simply glad to be around airplanes.

At the apartment, they couldn't convince her to come with them, so they left in search of food.

She changed into a skirt and blouse, let her hair down, made tea, had some bread and butter and an apple. She made a simple chart estimating the amount of money she'd get after the two shows tomorrow, and left a blank page for the amount she'd need for her own hangar and rent for airfield space.

The night was warm, with a cool breeze, so she took a sweater and a throw rug, and went down to the beach to write a letter to her father. She dropped the rug on the sand and sat on it. She relaxed, letting the sound of the waves drift through her, and the smell of sand and sea invade her senses. A string of lights along the esplanade cast a dim glow around her.

She watched the waves crashing and spilling foam which raced toward her. The wave crests glistened in the moonlight, and the rhythm of their rising, peaking, and breaking almost mesmerized her. Suddenly Johnny's eyes, looking into the depths of her heart, seemed to stare back at her from the waves. She knew she'd have to take time to think about what had happened when their eyes had spoken, but not now.

She picked up her tablet and pen. "Dear Father . . ." She'd left Nebraska two weeks ago, and so much had happened. She wasn't close enough to him to pour out her heart, but she corresponded regularly, at least to let him know where she was. He sent her brief notes, sometimes forwarding his sister Lulu's intriguing letters from around the world. She continued, "I'm in California . . ."

੨੦

Johnny and Curley went to a diner and ate the biggest meal on the menu.

"Boy, Miss Bailey is the berries! What a looker! Can she really do stunts?"

"I expect so." Johnny forked a piece of pie into his mouth.

"How old do you think she is?" Curley's boyish, friendly

face looked to him for an answer.

"Probably over twenty-one. A little too old for you." Johnny tried to remember when he was almost sixteen. That was just before he signed up for the War.

"Aw, I know she'd never have a crush on me." He shrugged and sat back in the booth. "But I can look up to her." He sighed. "She's swell."

Johnny picked up the check and they left. He took Curley home, then hurried home himself, hoping to see Meredith and ask her to go to church with him in the morning. But her apartment was dark. She had either gone out or was in bed early.

He stood for a moment, gazing at the dark apartment, then turned and looked out toward the sea. Too restless to go into his small apartment, he strolled across the sandy grass, crossed the boardwalk, and stood in the sand looking up into the black night dotted with stars. *God, if this is truly the girl for me, help me know what to do. She's very bold and headstrong.* That thought was quickly followed by another: *So are You.*

He turned his face to the clean breeze, and rubbed his arms against its coolness. *I have to get to know her better.*

ta

Meredith finished her letter to her father, telling him she had work but not saying exactly what. He didn't approve of her unladylike involvement with airplanes, and if he thought she was in a flying circus it would make his whiskers curl.

She laid the pad on the throw rug, rested on her arms, and stretched her legs out. Pensively, she looked out over the dark sea, thinking her father would probably like Johnny. She scolded herself for caring and for thinking of Johnny too often. Her life was starting, and she definitely did not have time for him. The best course, she decided, was to pretend he didn't exist and try to stay away from his charm that seemed too potent for her to keep resisting.

She realized she had a battle of personal restraint on her

hands. She was used to going her own way and being alone, so this was nothing new. Just a little more difficult than other times. But not impossible. "Mr. Johnny Westmore," she said to herself, "you're yesterday's news."

She drew up her knees and leaned forward, thinking that if she forced herself to imagine he was ugly or very old, it would be easier. *Yes,* she thought, *I'll imagine him as a nice hundred-year old man, and. . .*

Damp grains of sand sprayed her as a large figure dropped to his knees beside her. She stared at him wordlessly, trying her hardest to imagine him as ancient and frail. But the pounding of her heart thwarted the attempt.

nine

"Hello." Johnny grinned at her.

Her cheeks colored under his gaze, and she looked away, hoping he wouldn't notice. How could she imagine him as old and ugly, when his powerful, well-built body had just sank beside her with easy grace? His shoulders strained against the fabric of his shirt, she noticed and grimaced to herself.

She picked up the tablet and pen, and turned to him with a forced smile. "So, did you and Curley have a good dinner?" Reflected light from the sea glimmered over his handsome face. She tried to look away.

Johnny found himself leaning toward her. The wind flipped her ringlets around her face and neck. She looked ethereal and fragile in the moonlight. He drew back. "Sure did. You should have come with us."

They sat quietly for a few minutes, so comfortable words were unnecessary. She sighed, and started to get up. "Well, I have to get back. We've got a big day tomorrow."

He rose in one fluid motion and held his hand out to her. They walked close together, not touching. Her apartment was still dark. "Helen and her family must be having a good time," he said, opening the door for her.

She stood in the doorway. "Helen is good company," she said, keeping the conversation light. He made no attempt to move, so she took a step back into the room.

"How about going to church with me in the morning? We'll be at the field in plenty of time."

"I don't think so. We have to be there by eleven-thirty."

"We'll be there by eleven. I promise. My church has early

services." He folded his arms and leaned against the door frame.

Meredith paused, looked past him into the darkness, and said, "Thanks for offering, but no."

He nodded and looked down at her for a few seconds, then pushed away from the doorway. "All right. But one night soon, maybe we'll see the famous Aimee McPherson."

She couldn't argue with that. After all, she'd brought it up. "Maybe. Good night." She reached for the doorknob and stepped back. She had to escape from his hypnotic gaze and the attraction that was slowly causing her to forget her goals.

"Good night," he said with an endearing lifting of his brows. "See you at the field."

"At the field," she agreed and closed the door. She stood in the dark for a moment, restlessly stroking her chin. She was a complete failure at pretending he was unimportant. Every word, every gesture, and especially every look got her attention in a most alarming way, whether she wanted or not.

She walked across the moonlit room and turned the lamp on. She laid the tablet and pen on the table, then took the rug to the back door and shook the sand out. The activity felt good, and she shook the rug longer than necessary, thinking that she needed a good long talk with herself about the realities of her life.

She laid the rug out on the floor at the foot of her bed. *Remember who you are,* she told herself. *A woman trying to make a mark in a man's world. You have many months of struggle ahead, maybe years, just to get where a man can easily go. Think of the hard work, the grinding eyes-on-the-prize concentration you need.*

She sat on the bed. *Now think of how you'd feel if you fiddled your dreams away because some good-wlooking man captures your attention.* She wouldn't even imagine herself in any other position than standing in front of her own hangar with the "Bailey Flying School" banner draped above the door. If she lost her concentration now that she was on the first step toward her mark, she could lose it all. No man was worth it, not even the appealing Johnny Westmore.

She went into the kitchen, deciding to ask Meacham to move her booth next to Helen's, away from Westmore Aviation.

On a blank page she put a mark at the bottom, signifying her present position, wrote "Bailey's Flying School" at the top, and marked increments between the two. She opened her tool box, and fastened the sheet inside the lid. *There. That'll keep me from getting off track,* she thought. *Tomorrow I'll tape it to the side of the cockpit, where I'll see it every time I go up.*

❧

The next morning when she and Helen left, Johnny's car was gone. *He's at church,* she thought, frowning at unwanted memories of Pearl and herself seated in the front row of a chilly village church, while her father preached.

She and Helen arrived at the field to find Jim Meacham and Kate LaFore arguing loudly in front of the empty hangar. Helen and Meredith exchanged curious glances. They went straight to Helen's pinto-painted plane, where Joe busily buffed one spotted wing to a shine.

"What's that all about?" asked Helen.

With a wry glance in the direction of the hysterics, he said, "Jorge's gone and got hisself and the plane arrested. Runnin' rum from Mexico. Last night."

Meredith frowned. "So she has no plane for her act."

"Nope."

Helen pushed an errant pin into her coiled braid. "They'll be looking for someone to take her up."

"Not me," said Joe. "Meacham already tried. She called Pinto a motley old tub and said no."

Meredith watched Kate storm away from Meacham. He stood his ground and said a few words in a low voice that stopped her.

"Maybe he'll put her on one of those fighter planes," said Joe. "Where she belongs."

Meredith lost interest. "I've got things to do." She went into the hangar, hoping to talk to Meacham when he calmed down.

Slim and Tim, who were about sixteen years old, were there, bundling their parachutes. They grinned up at her. "Hello, Bird Lady," said Slim.

She had to smile. They looked guilty, as if she'd caught them at something. "Good morning. Are you planning something?"

They were always showing off for each other and for the crowds who loved them. They exchanged amused glances, laughed out loud, and Slim said, "Just watch us jump, and you'll see something interesting."

She agreed, and went to the back for her rolled-up sign. Outside, Meacham and Kate were talking quietly now.

Meacham glanced up. "Miss Bailey!" He beckoned to her. Kate stood pouting beside him. "Miss LaFore is in need of a plane for her act. How about it? Can you do it?"

Kate looked at Meredith beneath lazy, lowered lids, the queen condescending to tread upon a lowly oxcart. Meredith's good sense struggled with her desire to tell the darling Miss LaFore to go perform her tricks on a freight train.

Meacham gestured with both palms up. "Not the whole act. We just need to get her up for the crowd. All you'd do is fly low in front of them a couple of times, and she'll do the rest."

Meredith looked back toward Birdie, where Helen stood shaking her head. "How much does Jorge get for taking her up?"

Kate's eyes glittered with anger. "Find someone else!"

"Fine," said Meredith. "Bye!" With a little wave she started to walk away.

"Wait!" Meacham shot Kate a warning look. "I'll give you two hundred and fifty dollars for each show."

Meredith was barely able to control her joy. Five hundred dollars! The pampered Miss LaFore was turning red. "All right," said Meredith. "Providing I also perform."

Meacham looked skeptical. "Not that suicide dive."

"Agreed. And Sam announces me with all the flourishes."

"Right. You go right after Dancing Eagle. You'll be warmed up and ready." Meacham looked so relieved to have his star performer back in the show, he'd have agreed to anything, but Meredith didn't want to push it by asking him to move her booth too.

He nodded to them both, saying, "You two need to talk or take a practice run over at Venice Field, whatever you need to do." He hurried away, saying over his shoulder, "Miss Bailey, give Sam all the details before you go up."

"I don't need to practice, if you can fly straight," said Kate.

"Listen, I'm sorry about Jorge and your plane, but we'll be working together, so let's . . ."

"Be friends? You just keep your plane level, that's all I want from you."

Meredith met Kate's icy glare straight on. "I was going to suggest that we review your routine a couple of times before we perform. I barely glanced at your act yesterday."

"*I* perform. You keep the wings level."

How did this cold, angry woman transform herself into the lovely and graceful wing dancer?

Johnny hurried by with long, purposeful strides. He glanced at them and nodded. Kate LaFore's face was suddenly recast in a bright smile which faded the instant he passed. She showed Meredith the abbreviated routine, then walked off to change into her costume. Slim and Tim came out lugging their chutes.

Meredith went to find Sam. He was delighted to have another reason to work the crowd.

She hummed a happy tune, swinging her rolled-up sign as she briskly walked down the row of hangars toward Birdie. The only fly in the ointment was working with the irritable star.

Johnny stood beside his plane talking with Helen and Joe, and Curley lay on his back beside the tail skid. Helen ran toward her. "Merry! You're taking her up, aren't you?"

Meredith laughed in sheer joy. "Yes! But I made him promise to let me do my own stunts!"

Amazement touched Helen's bronze face. "You'll be going up three times! Once with me, once with Catty LaFore, and on your own!" She put her hand on Meredith's shoulder. "Little Sister, I don't know how you did it. But you're the cat's meow!"

"Shouldn't you say the wildcat's roar, or something Indian like that?"

Watching them approach arm-in-arm, Johnny admired the confident way Meredith carried herself, and he couldn't help noticing the enchanting way her laugh rippled through the air. He wondered what it would be like to have her laugh up into his eyes with such merriment.

Curley scrambled out from under the plane to hear Helen and Meredith announce the newest development. "It'll be keen! Miss LaFore, all dressed in white, on your purple plane!"

"Yes, it should be interesting," Merry agreed, and turned to leave.

Johnny watched her walk away. With her animation and small features, she didn't look much older than Curley. He dragged his gaze from her to find Helen thoughtfully watching him.

ten

When it was finally Meredith's turn, Curley cranked her prop, the engine burst into a roar, and she taxied into position for takeoff. She looked out over Birdie's vibrating wing toward the crowd. All heads were turned to her direction as they listened to Sam's larger-than-life description.

Her moment had arrived. She fed power to the engine and the plane rumbled over the grass, gathering momentum. She waved gaily the moment the vibration and bouncing stopped. Her wheels had left the ground.

The engine throbbed pleasantly. Her heart sang with elation as she climbed higher and higher. Her first stunt was looping the loop. She nosed Birdie into a dive to pick up speed, then climbed steeply, looped over backward, and dived again. Leveling out, she returned to the field, and turned upside down, flying low between the bleachers.

She did another loop close to the ground, which had the crowd cheering in relief when she pulled out of the dive mere inches away from disaster. She zoomed between the bleachers, rolling twice, straightened out, climbed into a half loop, followed by a half roll, which changed her direction, bringing her back overhead.

Johnny stood just inside the hangar door. From the shadows, he watched her cavorting about in the air. He balled his hands into fists, for a moment seeing not Meredith but Jeremy, his friend, dodging two attacking Fokkers over a field near France.

He slammed his fist against the door frame and walked out into the bright sunshine. The high-low roar of her engine took him back again. He pressed his hand against his forehead as the memories rose. "No," he groaned. "No."

He was crouched in a hole where the smell of death thickened the air and choked his lungs. He'd nursed his Spad fighter down to a rough landing and very nearly died just trying to get to the ground in one piece. He watched helplessly while two skilled German pilots, eager for the kill, relentlessly attacked Jeremy.

There was nowhere to hide in the sky, and Jeremy used every trick he knew to out-maneuver them, while firing back. Then a tracer bullet struck the fuel tank, and raw fuel surged against the red-hot whirling cylinders. It was over in seconds.

Johnny's pulse quickened as the fiery memory burned through his mind. He'd been able to keep from thinking about it for months. Whenever Jeremy came to mind, he thought of the good things. He took several deep breaths, remembered Jeremy's ease in telling a joke and his peals of laughter after he'd told one.

Still, a sadness lingered as he refused to look up, ignoring the sounds of Merry's plane gamboling about above him. He strolled over to the parts truck to check on business.

Meredith did a few more original stunts, then landed. The crowd was on its feet, waving, as she taxied down the runway. Waving back, she cut the engine and pushed up her goggles, astonished at the noise of their cheers.

She leaped from her plane and grinned at the hangars, at Helen, the sky, and the world in general. "I feel wonderful! I could pull the whole armada across Los Angeles by myself, if I wanted to!" she cried.

"I see your plane is down, but you haven't landed yet," said Helen, her hands on her hips.

"I hope I never do." She looked at her plane with great affection. "Birdie looks a little light on her wheels, too."

"And I hope you're still in seventh heaven after you've chaperoned the elegant Miss LaFore through her show."

"Helen, you're far more elegant than she is." Helen was impressive in her fringed buckskin jacket and skirt, her beaded headband, and soft moccasins laced up to her knees. When she started to protest, Meredith reached out and touched the red beads wrapped around the dark, shiny braid. "I mean it. You're a real Indian princess."

Two planes flew by, then Kate stood between the wings as Meredith took her up. Meredith had her hands full, keeping the sensitive Jenny steady as a hardwood floor, compensating for Kate's graceful moves across and between the wings.

When they landed, with Kate clinging to a strut with one arm, her other flung out in victory, the crowd was wild with applause. As soon as Meredith cut the engine, Kate leaped off and walked away with a flourish.

Helen laughed. "I think the crowd is applauding you more, but she doesn't know it."

"I don't care. I'm just happy to be up," said Meredith, lifting her gaze to the sky, where three planes circled above.

Helen's response was drowned out by the noise of their engines powering up.

"It's the jumpers," said Merry, shading her eyes against the glare. "Tim and Slim told me to watch for something special." They were too far away to hear Sam's shouted words, but when the jumpers leaped from the planes, one tumbled and flopped wildly through the air, rushing toward the ground.

Sam's voice fell silent, and the crowd watched in horror. "Somebody's hurt!" screamed Helen.

Meredith gripped Helen's arm, staring at the whirling arms and legs.

"He's gonna be killed," yelled Joe. Shrill screams rose from the crowd, and Sam's frantic shouts were punctuated by a sickening "whump," as the figure hit the ground. The ambulance, which was parked on the sidelines for the Dive of Death, raced to the spot, while Sam and some of Meacham's people kept the crowd back so the parachutists could land. Meredith, Helen, Joe, and others nearby scrambled over the grass to reach the poor soul.

The ambulance squealed to a stop, and the attendants stooped over the casualty. They looked up in stunned disbelief. Meacham pushed through the group, and hunched over a long moment, staring at the clothes stuffed with scraps.

"A pile of rags!" He gave a warning look at the group. "Whose idea was this?" Nobody said a word. He pointed to the mangled pants and jacket, and told the attendant, "Put it on a stretcher and take it away. Dump it somewhere and come back."

He walked quickly back to Sam, yelling that the jumper sustained minor injuries and would recover. The crowd moved restlessly, one group huddling around a woman who had fainted.

Helen and Merry glanced at each other and quickly walked away. Covering the beginning of a small smile, Helen said, "This must have been the 'something special' those young rascals told you to watch for."

Meredith watched Meacham make a beeline to the first chutist he could reach. "Uh-oh," said Meredith. "Meacham's not amused."

When the show was over, a large crowd converged in front of her plane, clamoring for rides. Meacham quickly made an appearance and upped the price, saying that the little lady had certainly shown her worth. Even at the new rate, she was unable to accommodate all who rushed at Curley with ten-dollar bills fluttering in their fists.

Curley kept Meredith's take in one box and Johnny's in another, while passing out Johnny's literature on air safety and passenger/goods transport.

Since there'd be no show following, the paid rides went on until dusk, when the aviators reluctantly had to turn away the people left waiting. For those who had their entrance tickets,

Meredith signed her initials, and promised they'd be the first to go up if they came to the show next Saturday.

Johnny watched in admiration. *She's certainly adept at handling herself and her business,* he thought. *She's given them incentive to come back not only to the Circus, but to her ride.*

Meacham came and picked up the cash while Curley, Johnny, and Meredith dismantled the makeshift booth.

"Good idea, signing ticket stubs for next week," said Johnny.

"Yep! You were swell!" said Curley.

"Thank you," she said with a radiant smile. Taking a short step toward Johnny, she said, "Mr. Westmore, may I talk with you for a moment?"

"Only if you call me Johnny." He cupped his hand under her elbow and drew her aside. He looked down into her eager face, noticing her lips' pink tinge.

"I'd like to rent tie down space beside your hangar."

He frowned and shook his head. "No need to pay me. You can tie down for as long as you like, no charge."

She lifted her chin and placed one hand on her hips. She gestured with the rolled-up sign in the other hand. "Five dollars a month. Either I pay you or I'll pay someone else."

A plane rumbled down the runway behind them, gathering speed for a takeoff. Johnny nodded his consent. "All right, but it's not necessary. You . . ."

"It is necessary," she said. "It's business—and it's important to me."

"Business," he said and stuck out his hand. She shook his and settled the deal.

"Now for un-business," he said, "would you like a ride to the meeting tonight?"

Striking the tie-down deal with him was about as close as she dared get, so she shook her head. "Thanks, but I'll ride with Helen."

He tilted his head and brushed the lock of hair from his

forehead. "I'll bring the extra overalls in case you want to make a hasty exit."

The vision of them rushing away on his motorcycle, the memory of her arms hugging him to hang on, slipped through her thoughts. She dragged her gaze from him, looking for any distraction in the dusky half light, and almost ran from him. "No thanks," she called back over her shoulder.

"See you later," he said quietly, though she was too far away to hear. Flicking a tuft of grayish-green grass back and forth with his toe, he looked down, wondering how he appeared to her. Had he been too bold? Or too aloof? Women these days were bolder, even sometimes asking men for dates. But Meredith didn't seem to be one of these. She didn't paint her face. Nor did she smoke or swear, and she hadn't yet bobbed her hair.

He shoved his hands into his pockets and in the growing darkness walked toward the hangars. He couldn't find fault with the fact that she was confident and full of strength and purpose. Beyond her determination and backbone, he sensed a sweet gentleness which she guarded closely.

He couldn't figure her out. At times she seemed to like him and other times she avoided him. *God, You're going to have to help me here.*

Curley and Ernie had the truck closed up and ready to go. *It'll soon be dark,* he thought, glancing at the hangar door where Meredith and Helen had gone to gather their gear. As if on cue, the door opened and they came out.

"Bye, Johnny," said Helen. To Meredith she said, "I'll pick you up in a few minutes." She started to walk away.

"Wait," called Johnny. "Pick her up where?"

"At your hangar, of course," replied Meredith, settling her leather cap on her head.

He waved Helen away. "I'm going there, too, so I'll take her home."

Meredith started to open her mouth to protest, but he shook his head quickly. "Please," he said softly. Helen and Joe waved and left.

"I needed to talk to Helen on the way home," she said with mounting impatience.

"I know you're settling your accounts, but there's something you need to know."

"What?" Instantly alert, Meredith looked intently at him.

"Come on," he said, leading her toward their planes. "Did you meet Helen's family yesterday?"

"Not really," said Meredith. "Why?"

"Her brother is here going to school, studying to be a teacher. His wife works at the phone company to help support him. But he and Helen have a mother and five or six other brothers and sisters in Arizona." He ducked under his plane's wings and circled it, looking up to examine seams and fasteners. She followed him, listening closely.

"Helen sends almost everything she makes to them." He stopped, and she almost bumped into him. "Just the extra gas it would take to drive to my field and pick you up would buy them a meal."

Disconcerted, Meredith crossed her arms and looked away. "I didn't know."

He walked toward Birdie. "I know you didn't." He ran his hand over the elevator toward the tail, and looked across the back of the purple plane at her. "There's something else, but—" He didn't want to put Helen in an embarrassing situation, so he just said, "Just don't offer to share the rent with her."

"Of course, I'll pay my share of the rent! I'm using the apartment, and it's only right!" She ran her hands over Birdie's side up to the lower wing.

He followed, stooping to check the tail skid. "She won't accept it."

Merry tested the wire tautness and circled to the engine. "And how do you know she won't?" She pulled the rag from her pocket and reaching up on tiptoes, wiped a smudge of oil from the exhaust pipe. "If she needs it as much as you say, she'll surely accept it."

Johnny reached up and stopped her hand. She could feel his warmth close to her back. She lowered their hands and turned. He stepped back a little, but not enough for her comfort. She ducked behind the propeller, to the other side of her plane.

He followed. "Just don't offer it, all right?"

"If you won't tell me a good reason, I'm going to talk to her about it tonight."

"You'll embarrass her if you do." His blue eyes surveyed her kindly. "Please trust me on this."

She shifted impatiently from foot to foot, looking up at him and trying to read his thoughts. She bent down and ran her hand over the wheel, thinking hard.

With a flash of insight she stood so quickly she almost hit her head. She gave him a sidelong glance. "You don't charge her rent, do you?"

He shrugged and slid his hand up one of the struts. "Just don't mention rent to her," he muttered.

Meredith peered at him until he glanced at her. She grinned at him and said, "You don't, do you?"

He rolled his eyes and looked away.

"I see." Elated by guessing his secret, she felt generous. "You didn't tell me, so your honor is intact. I won't mention rent to her."

"Get in. I'll crank." He looked up at the darkening sky.

"Yes sir, Mr. Tough Guy," she said, ducking under the plane to her foothold on the other side.

Johnny turned her propeller, and she rumbled over the grass for her takeoff. He then anchored his tail skid, got his engine running, loosed the skid, climbed in, put his plane in gear, and rose into the air behind her.

After they landed at his airfield, she followed him to his car. All the way home she kept him at a distance with her playful mood.

"So, from where did you come from on your trip to Los Angeles?" he asked.

She looked at him with a sparkle in her green eyes and her mouth curving into a small smile. "The Bible Belt!" she said, trying to suppress a giggle.

By the time they reached the apartments he was frustrated that he still knew practically nothing about her. How could he, when she laughed off his questions?

Meredith thanked him for the ride and didn't wait for him to open her door. She got out and ran into her apartment. She heard bath water running and said loudly to the door, "I'm home!"

"Good," said Helen. "I'll be out in a minute."

"Don't hurry," called Meredith, grateful for a chance to pull herself together. Her heart was racing, and she was short of breath. She stretched her fingers and arms, taking deep breaths. She leaned her head back and looked up at the ceiling, amazed at how silly she'd been, trying to cover her nervousness.

She sat on her bed, thinking. Her odd feelings had begun when she found out he'd not charged Helen rent. That was such an utterly kind gesture and his refusal to admit it bordered on chivalry. His concern for Helen's feelings touched her emotions deeply—and her unexpected response to his physical touch baffled her. So, in the confusion and turmoil of her thoughts, she simply laughed to ease the tension.

She had a lot to think about regarding Johnny Westmore. But first, she needed to concentrate on the meeting and dinner at the mansion. The days since the last meeting seemed a lot longer than a week. She'd have to put her thinking cap aside until she was back at the apartment again.

Later, when Meredith and Helen entered the spacious room, the band played "She's Only a Bird in a Gilded Cage," and the group laughed good naturedly. During the meeting Meacham congratulated Meredith on being instantly ready to fill in and assist Kate LaFore with her act. "You're a real team player," he said with admiration. He asked her if she had any other ideas for her act. Meredith told him a couple, and he approved them.

Kate sulked throughout most of the meeting, but she promised to have either Jorge back by the next week or another aviator to take her up. Meacham wanted her whole act, and she smiled with smug satisfaction. "Of course. The crowd expects excellence, and from me that's what they get."

Meacham offered to congratulate the brilliant person who sent the pile of rags to the ground, and when no one owned up to it, he threatened to fire all the chutists. In the end, he had to admit that it was a good idea, but he should have been warned beforehand. Slim said, "Does whoever did it want to do it again?"

Tim grinned and added, "If not, we will."

Meacham eyed them suspiciously when no one spoke up. They looked back in wide-eyed innocence. "Okay," said Meacham. "You take care of it next week. But we'll do it only occasionally. Every week and the crowd will figure it out, and it won't be a shock any more."

Johnny watched with pride as Merry accepted congratulations modestly. He was glad Jorge wasn't there to leer at her. He kept his eye on her without seeming to do so, and when the meeting turned into a full-fledged party, he advanced across the room toward her. Ernie and another mechanic intercepted him to get his opinion about installing cockpit instruments in an old Fokker. By the time he looked for her, she and Helen were saying their good-byes at the door.

She didn't need a ride home. He found Curley, drinking root

beer, playing checkers in a corner with one of the young chutists. "You and Ernie going pretty soon?" he asked.

Curley looked up from the board. "As soon as he gets that Fokker for sure."

Johnny nodded and left, riding down the driveway alone and wishing she were behind him. He decided to take her to dinner and church on Wednesday night.

eleven

On the way home, Meredith waved her bank draft in front of her face and laughed in pure joy. "A few more of these, and I'll be in business!"

Helen nodded and chuckled at her. "If anyone can do it, you can. Remember, there's another hundred dollars from me, for your part in my act."

Meredith wiggled back into the seat, shaking her head. "No, no, no. I didn't do that much. Besides, I learned something. I've never flown a wingwalker, and taking you up was instruction I used for Miss LaFore's act."

"A deal's a deal," Helen insisted.

"All right," said Meredith. "We'll put the hundred dollars in an emergency box, so it'll be there for either of us, just in case."

"In case of what?"

"Anything!"

Helen drove through the dark streets, while Meredith tried to think up a distinctive gift for her riders. "So they'll remember me, like your feather reminds riders they were with you," she said.

"Make it purple, the color of your plane," suggested Helen.

They talked about ribbons, purple-framed certificates, dyed feathers, a lavender business card with a plane drawn on it, a toy propeller she could initial, and other ideas.

Nearing home, Helen said, "Little Sister, I really enjoy having you stay with me."

"And I appreciate it, too. I don't know where I'd be if you hadn't invited me."

"The place is small, but you're welcome for as long as you wish. I hope it's a long, long time." She headed the car into the parking area and stopped. After turning the engine off, she moistened her lips and turned to face Meredith. "I don't want any money for you staying with me."

Meredith didn't know what to say. She shrugged one shoulder. "Well . . ."

Helen put her hand up to stop her. "Wait. There's something—" She rested her left hand on the steering wheel and gazed through the windshield. "But—"

"Anything!" said Meredith, sitting on the edge of her seat. "What?"

Helen took a deep breath and faced Meredith with a small glow in her eyes. "Teach me to fly?"

Meredith happily sank back. "Oh yes! My first student!" she said. "I'm thrilled! But why were you hesitant to ask?"

Helen locked her hands together in her lap and said solemnly, "It's a lot to ask, and I can't pay you."

"Don't you see?" said Meredith, "You're giving me a chance to learn how to teach!" She laid the bank draft on her open palm, and made invisible notes on it. "Lesson one: All about the airplane. Or should it be: How to start the engine? Definitely the airplane itself comes first." She looked up from her notes, smiling with satisfaction.

"Thank you," said Helen.

"No, thank *you*! Let's start tomorrow!"

They got out of the car, just as Johnny's motorcycle roared up beside them. He wheeled it onto its stand and turned the collar of his jacket down. "You two look happy," he said.

"We are," they said in unison and laughed.

"I'm in a festive mood," he said. "How about helping me eat some chocolate cake my mom sent home with me this morning?"

They rubbed their stomachs and groaned. "We just ate at the

mansion!" said Helen.

"Then let's all take a walk down the beach."

"You two go ahead," said Helen. "I have to call my brother."

Merry followed her. "And I have to plan gifts for my riders."

Johnny's eyes, under arched brows, were bright with challenge. "Tell me as we walk. Maybe I can help."

"Thanks, but I have to do it myself."

She turned again to leave but was stopped by his grip on her elbow. "Please. Just a short walk. I don't want to walk alone tonight." He lowered his hand from her elbow and looked at her with an expression of expectancy.

Every time he looked at her in that right-to-the-heart way, she felt a warm glow that puzzled her. She found herself smiling back at him and saying, "All right." She slipped her bank draft into her pocket.

"Good!" He stepped aside so she could precede him through the parking area to the boardwalk.

They walked past dark beach umbrella stands, cafes, most of which were closed, and waved to an old couple sitting on their porch, watching the waves. A couple strolled by hand in hand.

Johnny enjoyed having her with him. But he needed to know her better. "Look. The tide is coming in." He pointed to their left, where the water ran up to and passed the dark stain left by the previous wave. "I've seen you sometimes out here on the sand. You really like the ocean, don't you?"

"I sure do," she said. "Being alone on the beach, with the sound of the wind, and waves breaking is so, um . . . mighty, and peaceful too."

"I know what you mean." He studied the insolent scramble of curls on the top of her head. "Did you grow up near the coast?"

She tilted her face up and looked into the past. "We moved around a lot when I was young," she said. "I always liked the ocean smells." She inhaled deeply.

They walked in silence, then she stepped off the boardwalk. "Let's walk in the sand." Skipping, she called back to him, "Let's run!"

They ran near the water, dodging the incoming waves. They leaped over a narrow creek winding its way to the sea and ran for a long way.

Panting with exertion, Meredith leaned gratefully against a large rock and looked back where they'd been. To her right was the broad darkness of the sea. On the left an uneven line of lights winked at them. "Our footprints are being erased," she said.

"Yes. But some things never fade away."

"Like this rock!" She said, smiling up at him.

Her pale skin glowed in the soft moonlight. Resisting the pull drawing him toward her, he reached down and picked up a piece of driftwood and flung it toward the sea. It soared out over the water, and its fall into the ocean was obscured by the noise of the rolling surf.

"Do you like it out here?" he asked.

"If you mean California, yes." She watched for the drift-wood to bob up on the crest of the next wave. "But right here it's getting chilly." She hugged herself against the cool night air.

He shrugged out of his jacket and put it around her shoulders. "Let's start back."

There were fewer lights and nobody on the beach as they made their way back to the apartments. His jacket sat on her shoulders like a warm caress. She pulled it off and handed it back to him, suppressing a slight shiver. "Thanks. I'm not cold anymore." She scolded herself for enjoying this little walk entirely too much. How did she get talked into this, when she'd decided to steer clear of him?

"Tell me about your ideas for gifts for your riders," he said, interrupting her thoughts.

Glad to be back on the subject of business, she told him the ideas she and Helen had thought up.

"I like the initialed toy propeller and ribbon. You could promote your color by tying a purple ribbon to it."

"I'll think about it." Shivering, she eyed his jacket, hanging loosely in the crook of his arm, and almost snatched it back. Instead, she walked faster, swinging her arms as if the night was balmy. "Where were you born?" It was her turn to ask questions, and she managed to keep the conversation fixed on him for the remainder of their walk.

Back at the apartment, they stood under the porch light while he finished telling her about the time when he was boy when he and Nate had gotten a job following the ice cart to feed the horses. They had ended up getting lost in Cincinnati.

She enjoyed the story, and she noticed he seemed to have a lot of affection for his brother.

"You'll have to meet Nate and his family some time," he said.

Her natural enjoyment of meeting people almost caused her to say yes, but the image of her flying school rose up, and she knew she shouldn't be distracted.

Johnny could almost see her mind working. "I know you'd like them," he added.

"Maybe some time." She opened the screen door.

That was what she'd said about church. This was his chance. "How about coming to church with me Wednesday night?"

"I'm very busy, really," she said, shaking her head.

"You do believe in God, don't you?"

She squared her shoulders and her eyes flashed angrily. "Going to church or not has nothing to do with whether I believe in God."

"True, but believing in God does have something to do with whether you go to church or not."

In the tense silence that surrounded them, she thought of

her father saying something like that to her long ago.

He finally said with great sincerity, "I hope and pray you do believe in God, because no matter how good an aviator you are, anything can happen up there in the sky, and your life is on the line every time you take off." He stood quietly and didn't change his position as she turned and walked into her apartment.

After a moment, Johnny went back to his apartment and got down on his knees, questioning whether God had really picked her as the one to be his wife. "She's pretty and likeable, but she became hostile when I mentioned You," he prayed.

When Meredith walked in, Helen was seated on the sofa working the Sunday crossword puzzle. She looked up with a big smile. "You were gone a long time! Must have been a good walk."

"Hmph!" Meredith flopped down on the other end of the sofa. "He's a blowhard." While Johnny talked to God about her, Meredith talked to Helen about him.

Helen's dark eyes twinkled as she watched Meredith fume. "He likes you, you know."

Meredith narrowed her eyes and pursed her lips in disbelief. "You're wrong."

"No, I'm not. I saw the way he was looking at you today. He's smitten." She looked back at her puzzle. "No doubt about it."

Meredith put her hand over the puzzle. "You and he cooked up this walk tonight, didn't you?"

Helen moved one of Meredith's fingers. "I had nothing to do with it. That was your decision."

Meredith lifted her hand from the paper. "Well . . ."

"He's a nice guy. What happened out there that got you so upset?"

"Nothing," she said, standing up and going to the bedroom for a sweater. She came back into the room, pulling it on. "Let's talk about something else."

"Something must have happened. What was it?"

Ignoring Helen's insistence on the subject, Meredith said, "Let's talk about you, Helen the flyer."

Helen looked up with amusement creasing the lines around her eyes. "You're evading the subject," she teased.

Meredith walked to the door and turned. "If you won't talk about yourself, let me tell you about a lady named Bessie Coleman," she said. "That woman can fly! She didn't let the black color of her skin stand in her way."

Helen's blank look made Meredith laugh. "She barnstorms up and down the east coast, earning money to start her own school."

"A colored woman?"

Meredith had her full attention now. "I thought I had it hard, being a woman and no one would teach me to fly. But Bessie learned against greater barriers than I had—and she told me that you can do anything you want to, if you keep trying."

"Does she have her own school now?"

"Not that I've heard, but she's close."

Helen sat back, looked at the ceiling, awed. "Then an Indian woman could fly, too."

"Of course." Meredith sat beside her.

"I just want to fly, not stunts or anything. I want to feel the freedom of wings in the air."

Meredith smiled in encouragement. "I know. It's the most wonderful feeling. No one can explain it."

❧

The next two weeks went by in a flurry of activity as Meredith kept her mind on business. She bought food for the shelves, paid Johnny half a month's rent, worked on the small gifts for her riders, and planned newer, scarier stunts. She practiced her routine, and gave Helen her first lesson. She had considered finding another field to tie Birdie down, but she'd been able to avoid Johnny, so she didn't pursue that option.

By word of mouth her fame had spread, and her stunts were wildly applauded. She realized that part of her popularity was because she was the new act in the show, but it was also because she dared to do some risky new tricks, including what she called a "wing twist" loop, in which at the top of a vertical bank the plane rolled wing over wing. She drafted Slim and Tim and gave each one a straw hat with a purple scarf tied around it. With hooks attached to the wing skids, she flew low between the boys, who held the hats up. The hooks snatched them, and she ascended with the scarves streaming behind as victory banners.

Johnny's business kept him working late most nights, and though he tried to find a moment with Meredith, he was unable to get her attention. After the shows, they were both swamped with riders, and she seemed to disappear before he could talk to her.

She was avoiding him, and he was reluctant to track her down. Two weeks later, though, an idea came to him for getting her to both see him and go to church. At Wednesday night church, his brother had mentioned that a nearby church's advertised Sunday sermon was something about getting to heaven on a flying machine. Surely, that would get her attention.

That same night, Meredith and Helen made a vegetable soup from fresh vegetables they'd bought. After they finished the dishes, they worked at the table. Helen tied a bead and leather strand to each feather. Meredith pored over her account sheet with pleasure. In only four weeks she'd earned enough to put her onto the first step of her line from the bottom of the page to the Bailey Flying School Banner at the top. It was November, and if all went well this month and next, she'd have enough to start looking for her own hangar. Maybe she'd even buy a car.

The small kitchen was quiet. Helen's beads clinked against each other when she reached in to get one, and Meredith's pencil scratched across the paper as she figured how many shows were left in the year and approximately how much money she'd earn by December 31.

Two shows on Saturday and two on Sunday. The first Sunday show didn't start until eleven, and if a church were near the field, she could go and get to the show in time.

"Helen, do you ever go to church?" she asked.

Helen slipped a bead onto the leather string. "Sure, when I was a kid. Some missionaries came out to the reservation." She cut the string and tied the end of it into a tight knot. "And I went with Johnny once or twice." She reached into the box for a feather. "Do you?"

"I haven't in a long time, but—" She shrugged one shoulder. "I don't know . . ."

Helen nodded. "With two shows on Sunday and the meeting afterwards, there's no time."

Meredith absentmindedly traced the edge of the paper with the pencil, and sighed. "Yes. That's right."

Restlessly, she got up and stood looking out the back window at the stars, thinking how wonderful it would be to fly over the ocean in the moonlight.

A knocking at the door interrupted her daydreaming. "I'll get it," she said.

Johnny stood on the porch, holding the screen door open with one hand. In the other he held a sack. "Cookies," he said with a smile.

"Who is it?" called Helen behind her.

"Johnny Westmore." Meredith stepped back, wondering why he was here. "Come in," she said.

He came in, set the sack of cookies on the table, and opened it. "My mother made these."

Meredith avoided his eyes that probed and mesmerized her. She hoped Helen wouldn't notice anything odd about her behavior.

Helen got up to make a pot of coffee, while Johnny admired the feathers and beads. They chatted about the circus, airplanes, and flying.

"Merry's teaching me to fly," said Helen, leaning forward in her chair.

His eyebrows raised in inquiry. "You're going to get off the wing and into the cockpit?"

Helen shook her head, laughing. "I'll leave tricks to the experts. I just want to get off the ground and move through the clouds."

"Is it everything you thought it would be?" Johnny flicked a brief glance at Meredith, then looked back at Helen.

She closed her eyes with bliss. "More," she breathed. "Much more."

There was something different about Johnny tonight, observed Meredith as they talked. He had the usual intensity of purpose that was a natural part of him, but tonight he seemed happier, more certain.

They broke the last cookie into three pieces and finished it off. Johnny put down his cup and said, "Come to church with me Sunday."

"We were just talking about that!" exclaimed Helen.

"You were?"

Meredith nodded. "And we agreed that it's impossible, in light of doing two shows that day."

He told them the title of the sermon and promised to get them to the field on time. Helen and Meredith were intrigued, but decided against going.

Johnny appeared to accept their decision, but his eyes darkened briefly with disappointment, and Meredith felt a prick of guilt. "Maybe a midweek service," she said.

"I'll count on it," he agreed, getting up and putting his cup in the sink.

Meredith followed him to the door, sorry to see him leave.

He stepped out onto the porch and she stepped out beside him. He stood quietly, evidently deep in thought. A warm Santa Ana breeze blew across her shoulders.

"Would you like to walk on the beach?" he asked.

Thoughts of strolling beside him on the sand were tempting. She looked up at the stars. "It's a beautiful night," she said wistfully.

"Or maybe a drive," he added. "It's too nice a night to waste."

She was finished with her work, she'd balanced her accounts, and had her plans for the next two months firm in her mind, so she felt that a drive, just this once, wouldn't hurt.

twelve

After their moonlight ride, Meredith relaxed, settling into a more easygoing rapport with Johnny. She still, however, avoided being alone with him in what she called "distracting predicaments," such as romantic walks in the sand and heart-to-heart talks.

That Sunday, she performed a new stunt she'd been practicing all week. After picking up the scarves held out by Tim and Slim, she climbed to three thousand feet, cut the switch and did loops and wing overs with a dead engine. The engine coughed a few times before going back to work, and then she triumphantly flew upside down between the bleachers, within yards of the ground. The crowd's relief at her escape from certain death resulted in wild cheers and enthusiastic waving to her when she landed.

When Johnny heard her engine quit, he looked up from replacing a faulty engine switch. He held his breath, praying she'd avoid going into a spin. When he heard the engine start again, he breathed out in relief and went back to work.

When the same thing happened during the second show, he was sipping hot coffee. He almost burned his mouth when he choked it down, realizing that she deliberately cut the engine to shock the crowd. He coughed and gulped deep breaths of cool air.

Ernie stuck his head out of the cockpit where he was working and said, "Coffee gone down the wrong pipe?"

"Something like that," gasped Johnny, frowning. He stalked out of the hangar and watched her gaily whiz down the field upside down. When she finally taxied to a stop, he was there.

Meredith climbed out of her plane and leaped to the ground in triumph. She tilted her head to remove her goggles. "They loved it!" she exclaimed, joy shining in her eyes.

Johnny stared at her with a frown of cold fury. "Do you know what could have happened if your engine hadn't started?"

She looked up into his dark, angry face, bewildered for a moment. Laughing off her annoyance, she said, "I'd have landed somehow."

His strong hand reached out and grabbed her arm. "Last year one hundred and seventy-nine barnstormers who thought they were invincible were in accidents, and eighty-five were killed." He glared at her. The force of his eyes, blazing blue fire, threw her off guard. She bit her lip and looked away. "Are you smarter than Locklear or Beachey?" he asked. "They were supposedly the best."

She pushed his hand from her arm. "I'm fine! I told you before, I'm in complete control. Anyway, why do you care?"

Curley, Helen, and Joe converged on Meredith to celebrate her daring stunt. Johnny didn't get to answer her question. He walked away with a warning cloud on his features.

"What's the matter with him?" asked Helen.

Struggling to maintain an even, unconcerned tone, Meredith shrugged, saying, "He didn't like my stunt."

Curley couldn't stand still. "You were fabulous!"

Helen thoughtfully watched Johnny walk away. "We all were afraid you were in trouble." Joe nodded in agreement.

"But I wasn't," Meredith said irritably.

Johnny clenched his jaw as he strode away from them. "Lord," he muttered, "I'm trying hard to get to know this girl, but I can't take much more. She won't come to church, she flings herself around in the sky risking her life, and only talks about unimportant things. Find someone else for me, please!"

He paused just inside the door of the hangar, trying to dispel the image of her smiling face, the color whipped into her cheeks by the wind, and her eyes that flashed with energy and fire.

That night at the gathering in the mansion, Johnny passed a group caught up in happy banter about the good old days of barnstorming around the country. Meredith was in their midst, laughing and regaling them with her story of the time she used the cows in a field as a weather vane. They'd turned their tails to the wind, so she landed accordingly. "But the rascals licked the dope from the wings when I wasn't looking, and I had fabric sagging like old rags beneath the spars."

One of the armada aviators, a youngish man with a dapper mustache, laughed, telling how he'd look for garages and land as close as he could, then carry gas to his plane, straining it through a chamois skin to keep water from his tank.

Before he finished, a tall, blonde aviator said he added moth balls to increase the performance of his engine.

Johnny wondered if Meredith could see that they were trying to impress her. He started to walk away, when one of the men said, "Westmore! You must have some stories from the good old days." They looked at him, smiling. "Hector here just told us how he sealed a leaky radiator by pouring in bran with the water.

Meredith looked like a golden flower in the midst of their dark clothes. She wore that dark yellow dress he'd seen her in the first night she came here. Tonight, however, she didn't have the close-fitting hat on, and her hair surrounded her laughing face like a red-gold halo. "Yes, Johnny, join us."

A trace of laughter in her voice challenged him. Their faces were friendly, welcoming him with smiles, but her smile was the one that drew him. "I was in the War, and there isn't much amusing to tell about those days." The smiles faltered. His gaze came to rest on Meredith's questioning eyes.

Putting the War aside with good humor, he said, "I had a friend in the Love Field Lunatics. He had a wing walker who climbed a seven-foot ladder atop the upper wing. As my friend started into a loop over a state fair in Dallas, the wing walker fell off and tumbled into the cockpit right on top of him."

Meredith smiled up at him. He answered her smile with one of his own and continued, "One of his pants legs slipped over the control stick. There he was, his flying controls up the walker's pants leg. He told him, 'Don't move, and I'll try to land by holding on to your leg and the stick, too.' They made it."

Heads shaking in disbelief and laughter, they all agreed— this was the best business in the world. "To me, it is a business," said Johnny. "Think about it! The War is over, and the airplane is here to stay, not as a freak sideshow thrill, but for real, honest-to-goodness service to everyone."

Meredith admired his camaraderie and gentle wit. He gave them a story as good as theirs, and while he had their attention, took the chance to tell them what he really felt about flying. He stood, tall and straight, dressed in black, gesturing with his strong, long-fingered hands, his compelling blue eyes looking into that aeronautic future only he could see.

"Picture this," he continued, "a plane that can carry ten, maybe even twenty people, all inside, taking them from here to—" He held up both hands, "Oh—San Francisco!"

One aviator cocked an eyebrow and said, "Suitcases, too?"

Johnny waved the comment aside as if nothing was impossible. "Of course. Some day there'll be airplanes that take only cargo, like trains or boats do now."

Someone commented, "I see how you could maybe close the cockpit, but there's no room for more than two people."

Others said, "They can ride on the wing!" And, "You could seat three on each wing." And, "What a way to take a trip!"

The blonde aviator asked, "Why don't you design such an airship, Westmore?"

He folded his arms and stepped back, looking intently at Meredith. "I just might," he said. She watched him walk away, nodding to another group as he passed them.

During the meeting, the owner of the house spoke, asking for three aviators for his latest movie. He ignored Meredith's raised hand and chose three men.

Johnny watched the tense set of her shoulders when the movie mogul passed over her, and he knew she was stung by the rejection. Now was the time to tell her what he had in mind to help her.

When the meeting was over, he approached her. "I'd like to talk with you for a moment."

She glared at him with burning eyes. "That man has a sixteenth-century mind!" she snapped.

"But he's making twentieth-century movies," he countered.

Meredith rolled her eyes, glancing back to where the man had stood and looked through her as though she didn't exist. "Well," she tossed her hair back with an air of defiance, "I don't need him anyway!" She suddenly seemed to realize Johnny stood before her, taking all this in. She met his eyes boldly, then the green fires in her eyes softened, and she said, "Sorry. It's nothing. You wanted to talk to me?"

"Let's go where we can talk." He offered his arm.

Once again, she found herself taking his arm and leaving with him, in spite of her good intentions to steer clear of him.

They walked to the same place where they'd talked the first night she'd arrived here. That seemed so long ago. "How was that sermon about going to heaven in an airplane?" she asked, then grimaced for bringing up the subject of church. She took surreptitious peeks at him. His black pants and jacket emphasized his lean, sinewy good looks.

"Oh, it wasn't at my own church, so I didn't go," he said, offering her the bench. "I teach an active group of ten-year-olds, so it's hard to get a volunteer to take them on when I'm not there."

They sat, and he leaned forward, looking at her intently.

"That trick you did today—twice—is very dangerous, especially with your OX-5 engine."

She started to protest, but he stopped her. "Hear me out. I know that engine. It has a nasty habit of acting up at all the wrong times. I've seen aviators barely make it back to the ground."

She frowned, wondering what he was getting at.

"I have a Hispano-Suiza, which would give you a lot more power and dependability."

"A Hisso!" She sighed, imagining the difference. Lots of Jenny owners replaced their engines with that one. "But it weighs more."

"Fifteen pounds. But you get nearly double the horsepower." He could see her expressive face weighing the possibilities. "It'd be safer," he added.

"I'll be able to climb three times as fast!" She grinned with pleasure.

Johnny stifled a groan and kept his face expressionless. "Remember safer?"

"Safety is my constant passenger," she said. "How much would this fabulous Hisso cost?"

He leaned back, resting one arm on the back of the bench, and said, "Twenty-five dollars."

She thought for a minute, weighing the loss of that much from her stash against the advantages of the more powerful engine. Envisioning her school, the newer, more powerful engine was in her best interest and that of her students too.

She accepted his offer and insisted on doing the work herself. Admiring her courage and determination, he agreed, pleased with the idea that she'd be around his hangar all day, even though he'd be gone a lot with his transport business. They shook hands on the deal, and went back to the mansion. He made a mental note to tell Ernie to keep an eye on her, to keep her from lifting heavy things. Curley would probably hover

over her, trying to put her on a velvet cushion while he did all the work. He smiled to himself, thinking how this determined, outspoken woman would handle that!

❧

The next morning Johnny woke up with the feeling that something wonderful was about to happen. He had to force himself to concentrate on his chapter in Romans. The insistent feeling of expectation distracted him each time he looked at the words. He finished the chapter and was praying for his family when Meredith's soft knock at the door interrupted him.

She stood on his porch in the cool morning air, curly wisps framing her face. A damp fog muted the sound of the waves behind her. Her tool box and seat beside her, she held her coveralls rolled up in one arm, and a basket with more tools in the other. Her face shone with the elation of a child about to embark on a long trip. "Be early, you said."

He opened the door and motioned her to come inside. "Right. I'll get my jacket and we'll be on our way." He had to turn away from her so she wouldn't see the smile he couldn't hide.

That first morning they went in his car, because of her tool box and basket. After that, they rode the motorcycle.

Johnny must really enjoy his work, thought Meredith. *He certainly seems happy.*

No matter how early they got to the hangar, Ernie was already there. He nodded when Johnny brought her in Monday morning. Johnny explained that she'd be installing the new engine in her Jenny.

Curley's face lighted with a big grin. "I'll help!" He reached for the basket she carried. "Here, let me carry this."

She swung her arm back a little, giving him an amused look. "Thank you, but I'm a big girl."

His face reddened, making the freckles stand out. "Oh." He stepped back from her. "Sure."

She turned away, looking at the empty space in the hangar,

pretending not to see his chagrin. Then she looked back at him and asked, "Where's the powder room or whatever you men call it? I need to get my coveralls on and get to work."

"Over here," said Curley, walking toward one of the corners. She put down her basket and followed him. Johnny slid open the hangar door, admiring the way she had showed her independence, yet still showed understanding for Curley's adolescent feelings. She allowed Curley to help her push Birdie into the hangar.

Ernie and Curley seemed amused when she asked them to treat her no differently than they would another man. But as she stood on her stool, handling her tools skillfully as she took off the propeller and cowling in order to remove the old engine, they began to relax around her. She soon felt comfortable working alongside them.

She felt good having her hands back in the engine, working to make Birdie faster and stronger. Sometimes she and Johnny discussed new planes, who was doing what in the aviation business. He brought a newsletter from the San Diego field, which gave her ideas for an advertisement for her school.

On Wednesday, Chad arrived, having ridden the trolley from school. His hair stood up in wisps from the wind blowing outside. "Is Uncle Johnny back yet?" he asked.

"No. He must be on a special trip," said Meredith.

"Maybe it's too windy and he won't come back." Chad stood at the front of Birdie's fuselage, looking up at the emptiness. "What's that?" he asked, pointing.

"That's the fire wall," said Meredith, tapping on her wrench to loosen a tight screw. "And no, it's not too windy. He'll be here." She'd met Chad before when he'd come to see Johnny, and she liked the dark haired boy with the deep-set eyes and charming freckles sprinkled across his small nose.

Chad quietly circled the plane, examined the engine which lay on the workbench at the side wall, then sauntered over to

Ernie who sat hunched over the valves he was grinding. Soon they heard Johnny's plane make its approach to land.

Chad obediently waited until he heard the engine quit, just as he'd been told to do, and then he ran out to meet Johnny, who grinned at the boy and ruffled his hair. "Hi, Tiger! How's my favorite nephew?"

Chad laughed. "How can I be your favorite? I'm your *only* nephew."

"That's it. My only and favorite nephew." He put his arm on the boy's shoulder as they walked. "How's Ace doing?"

"Boy, is he smart!" Chad stopped and stepped in front of Johnny, so he had to listen. "Sunday night he cornered a rabbit! He was barking like crazy when we got home from church."

"What happened to the rabbit?" Johnny knew his sister-in-law, who put small bugs outside rather than kill them, would defend the rabbit, even if it was enjoying her tasty garden.

"It got itself in a corner under the porch where Ace couldn't reach it, and it was just sitting there watching him bark." They entered the hangar. "Dad got him into a cage, and Nell wants to keep him and teach him tricks."

When the sky began to darken, Johnny walked toward Meredith. She leaned into the fuselage, carefully scraping with a small tool. He stood quietly, approving her mechanical competence.

She stopped scraping and looked over her shoulder at him. "Hello."

"Hello, yourself. Looks like you're about ready to put the Hisso in."

She turned around and wiped her cheek with the side of her hand, leaving a small dark smudge. "Tomorrow's the day!"

He balled his hand into a fist to resist the ridiculous urge to reach out and wipe the smudge away. "Good!" He rubbed his finger along a highly polished wood strut in a nonchalant way and said, "Care to come to church with Chad and me tonight?"

He pretended indifference, but she could tell her answer was important to him. She'd already turned him down twice, because she didn't want to get distracted from her goal. Now, she felt accepted as just another mechanic, and he was a co-worker and friend, no more. "All right," she said, pushing back a nagging little voice that laughed at her denial of attraction.

She looked down at her coveralls. Underneath she wore trousers. "Oh. I can't go in trousers!"

Perplexed, Johnny scratched his head. "They'll understand." He frowned. He knew one woman who wouldn't. "God will understand," he said.

She shook her head. "No, I couldn't go like this. I'm sorry."

"We could take you home for a quick change . . ."

"Which way is the church?" she asked.

He frowned, regretfully admitting it was the other way.

"I'll go with you Sunday," she promised. "If you guarantee to get me to the field in plenty of time before the first show."

A satisfied light glowed in his eyes. "You have my word on it." He rewarded her with his devastating grin. "Ernie will take you home. See you in the morning!"

"Good-bye!" She climbed back onto her stool and glanced through the wires as he walked over to Chad and Ernie. He looked back at her, but she quickly focused on what she was doing, pretending not to notice.

When she got home that night, Helen sat before a large bulls-eye with a paintbrush in her hand. "This stands up on the end of one wing," she gestured with her right hand, then looked the other way and gestured with her left hand, "and I stand on the other wing and shoot an arrow at it."

"It's a perfect stunt!" exclaimed Meredith.

Helen turned back to her bulls-eye with satisfaction. "There's a letter for you on the table," she said.

She recognized her father's writing, and opened the envelope slowly. He'd be pleased she was going to church Sunday, but she was glad he wouldn't know, though she felt guilty for the childish attitude of willfulness.

Her father's letter was short, stating that he was glad to finally hear from her and hoped she was well. Meredith finished the letter and gazed at the blackness filling the kitchen window. A lost, lonely feeling filled her for a moment. Then she jumped to her feet, pushing the loneliness out of her mind once more.

thirteen

Meredith brooded over her meager wardrobe. Her yellow dress and her blue skirt and white blouse were all she had besides coveralls, and she needed something new. She and Helen went shopping the next morning. They'd planned on going downtown, but traffic on Wilshire Boulevard convinced them to circle back to a department store they'd passed.

Meredith could hardly believe her eyes at the crowds of shoppers. Helen leaned out of the way of two women hurrying up the aisle toward a table with a large SALE sign hanging above it. The table was surrounded by women picking through the piled up clothing. "They think they save money by buying that which they don't need," said Helen.

It had been a long time since Meredith went shopping, and she decided it would be a long time before she went again. She longed to escape the confusion, back to the peace and quiet of the airfield.

They found the dress department, and she bought a navy blue jumper and a green silk dress, gathered below the waist, with a circle of lace around the collar. They both bought underwear, braving pushy shoppers for a sale on holeproof silk stockings.

Helen took her to Johnny's and went on to work on her bow and arrow stunt. Meredith allowed Ernie and Curley to help lift the new engine onto the motor mounts. She stood back, admiring the shiny metal. "It's beautiful!" she breathed.

"Fast, too!" agreed Curley.

"I can hardly wait to try it out!" She rubbed a spot of grease from her hands with a rag. "But there's a lot to do, even before putting the propeller back on."

She worked hard the next two days and finally had the plane ready for engine testing and tune-up late Friday morning. By three o'clock everything was checked and double-checked, and she was eager to see how the airplane would now perform in the air.

She taxied down the runway, and as soon as the wheels left the ground she had her familiar ecstatic feeling, only instead of the usual gentle climb, this time the aeroplane nosed up steeper and much faster. After about fifteen minutes, she almost shouted for joy at the engine's response to the throttle stick.

She climbed twice as high as she'd ever been, then did three loops in a row, just for the fun of it. She flew out over the ocean, turned upside down, and waved to a startled fishing crew.

Back at Westmore Field, she leaped from the plane, hastily pulling her goggles and hat off. She ran to the hangar, where Johnny stood leaning against the door watching her approach.

"I take it you like the new engine?" he asked.

She felt so light with excitement, she didn't feel the ground beneath her. She grabbed his hand. "The transformation is wondrous! First rate!"

"I knew you'd like it," he said, amused by her excitement.

She let go of his hand and looked back at Birdie, her purple paint shining brightly in the slanted afternoon rays. "This is as exciting as the day I first soloed."

"How was takeoff?"

Joy bubbled up, and she almost laughed. "Nearly straight up, and three times as fast!" Her glance fell upon the OX-5, and she had a feeling of disloyalty. She touched it gently. "This old engine has put in many wonderful miles and hours of flying. We've been through a lot together."

Johnny pulled out his watch and checked the time. "How do

you think the new engine would do on a long haul for Westmore Aviation?"

She looked back over her shoulder at him. "Are you commandeering my aeroplane?"

"I'm employing both of you. I need to get a package to Catalina Island as soon as possible. How about it?"

"Catalina Island?" She couldn't remember seeing it on her map.

"Twenty-six miles off the coast. A nice flight," he said. "And the payment will be a full tank of gas when we return."

She managed to keep her smile from becoming an out-and-out grin. "Right now I'd say yes even to a trip to New York!"

"Good! I'll show you where Catalina is." He motioned to the maps on the wall. He pointed out Catalina, their location, and landmarks along the way. "We'll land here, at the Blackhawk Ranch. I'll be your passenger."

He untied a large box from his motorcycle rack and carried it out to the plane. They filled the tank with gas, and were soon aloft in that new delightful steep climb that took her breath away.

She climbed to three thousand feet, banked to her left, and headed south, away from the city, which fanned out in all directions. Johnny caught her attention and pointed between the right wings to the afternoon sun lighting the clouds to a golden pink glow.

She flashed him a grin and almost did a loop right there, but she stopped herself, thinking of the package at his feet. Dumping his special delivery would not make him happy.

What did make Johnny Westmore happy? She recalled the times she'd seen him smile. He seemed to enjoy their impromptu picnic; and he obviously loved his nephew, judging by the happy smile with which he'd greeted him on Wednesday.

She flew on, over Palos Verdes, dipping the wing to get a better view of the lush greenery and the cliff that plunged to the pounding surf below. She had a sudden memory of the pleased look of admiration in his eyes when he picked her up for their picnic, then frowned at those thoughts. She wasn't interested in how he felt about her, she merely wondered what made him happy.

Concentrate, she told herself. Listen to the engine. It droned with a deeper throbbing than she was used to, but it sounded very, very good. She couldn't resist dropping altitude and happily circling around a boat sailing into San Pedro Bay. The boaters waved, and she waved back, noticing that Johnny even managed to stretch out his arm in a stiff wave.

Johnny sat in the front cockpit, beneath the top wing, a cat's cradle of struts and bracing wires stretching between the wings on either side of him. He looked down at the sailors waving so enthusiastically that he'd had to return the sentiment. Merry seemed energized by their presence, grinning and waving as if they were the only sign of life she'd seen in six months. A golden curl had escaped her cap and fluttered around her happy face. Obviously, her hair was as spirited as she was.

He was learning not to be surprised at anything this unpredictable woman would do, and he decided his cargo would be safer behind his feet, in case she decided to turn upside down or loop the loop.

He had not been a passenger for years in an aeroplane, and he felt odd. But he had to admit he felt no unrest with her at the controls. She was right when she told him she had perfect control of her aeroplane. He looked through the whirling propeller at the flat clouds below the sun and relaxed his shoulders against the seat.

Meredith slowed down and dropped slightly to get a closer look at Catalina, where sailboats clustered around a long pier. People strolled down a small street lined with gaily colored outdoor vendors. She continued on over the island, touched down, and rumbled over a cleared strip of land beside a large barn.

Three men, dressed in cowboy work clothes, ran toward them, followed by a dozen boisterous teenagers. One of the men took the box, explaining that the owner's daughter's seventeenth birthday party started soon at a secret location, only arrived at by a moonlit hay ride. While hauling hay, the wagon broke down, and the box contained bearings and bolts to fix it.

He paid Johnny, thanked him, and carried the box back to the barn. The young people clustered around Birdie, and one girl with her foot in the foot-hole leaned inside, peering at the controls.

She looked at Johnny with wide eyes and said, "I *love* your aeroplane! Why is it purple?"

Johnny raised an eyebrow in amusement and nodded to Meredith. "The plane belongs to her. Ask her."

Meredith talked briefly with the awe-struck girl, then offered her a birthday ride. She took the delighted girl up, then when everyone wanted a ride, she offered to show them some stunts instead and did some slow rolls and loops for them. When she taxied back onto the runway, they cheered and thanked her, then ran off for their party.

For the first time, Johnny enjoyed watching the grace and skill with which she rolled and glided through the air. For the first time in his life, he didn't feel his fists clench in anger at the stupid antics of daredevil idiots. Instead, he began to see an aeronautical future where there'd be room for both cargo and passenger service—and the individual aviator who took to the air for pleasure and personal travel, in safer planes.

But he didn't fool himself about the inherent danger in what Meredith was doing. Aeroplanes were unpredictable, killing many good aviators. Even her new engine, though it gave greater speed and maneuverability, was not perfect, and she could encounter difficulties at any time. He hoped and prayed she'd be able to land when trouble happened.

But for the moment, she rumbled toward him, the engine

idling sweetly. He sauntered toward her. "Going my way?" He looked up into eyes shining with delight. He could get used to basking in the brightness of those eyes.

"Get in and hang on!" she called. They took off and headed west, instead of east. She swooped low over a cove on the western side of the island, then landed on a grassy bluff about fifteen feet above the beach.

"Rosalie, the birthday girl, told me about this place," she said. "There's an old seal here named Oscar. He's friendly, and he'll eat anything you throw to him." She reached into a pouch sewn to the underside of her wicker seat. "I always have a few crackers, in case I get hungry."

"I think seals eat fish," said Johnny, laying his cap on the seat as he climbed out of the cockpit.

They stood for a moment in the tall grass, enjoying the fabulous sunset and almost other-worldly quality of this secluded beach. Meredith shaded her eyes, looking out over the silvery dazzle of sun on water, searching for seals. The only sound was the breaking waves and the calls of gulls wheeling overhead.

"Come on!" She walked and slid down the bank, running the short distance to the edge of the foaming waves.

Johnny took off his shoes, which were rapidly filling with sand, and she did the same. "Maybe if we did a seal call, he'd come," he said, tossing their shoes safely back from the water.

She laughed. "In England they bark like old dogs."

"It's the same here," he said, rolling his pants legs up above his ankles.

Meredith held up the crackers, shouting above the noisy sea, calling all seals to step right up for the tasty treats. After a few minutes, when a seal failed to appear, she tossed half a cracker on a receding wave. It disappeared beneath the head of an incoming wave, then bobbed up on top of the surf, to be gobbled up by a gull.

Johnny enjoyed her attempts to lure a seal. She seemed unaware of his presence. He was enchanted by her playfulness, a side which he hadn't yet seen. Her usual attitude was that of proving she was as competent in the machine shop as any man. Today she moved across the wet sand with the grace of a frolicking child.

The sun poised on the horizon clouds, ready to sink beneath sea level, casting long shadows behind them. Suddenly she pointed out to sea. "What was that? Some bird dived straight into the water!"

A brown bird floated on the swells fifty yards away. "It's a pelican," he said. "They dive for fish."

"If there are fish here, where's Oscar?"

"Good question," he said, looking up the coastline. "Maybe looking for better hunting at the next cove."

"Too bad for him!" She broke the crackers and tossed them into the midst of a group of gulls, scattering them for a moment until they realized the white objects were food. "It's getting late," she said, squinting at the horizon. "We'd better go."

They picked up their shoes and started up the sandy incline, Meredith ahead of him. Near the top, she took too big a step, slipped, grabbed at a tuft of grass, and tumbled back.

He braced himself and caught her in his arms. His cheek pressed tightly against the back of her shoulder for an instant. She smelled faintly of violets and soap. She felt warm and soft and wonderful. "Are you okay?" he asked, his voice husky.

"Fine," she answered, pulling away from him slightly to look up into his face.

Johnny looked down into those eyes, the green fire in them now a soft muted glow. Her steady gaze looked back at him, and he couldn't look away. He was drawn into the depths of her eyes, as if they were magnetized. He felt almost a reverent sense of peace pass through him and a stillness that blocked out the sounds of the sea and birds, leaving only his heartbeat, which seemed to thunder in his ears.

Meredith took a moment to catch her breath. When Johnny asked if she was okay, he sounded as if he'd had the wind knocked out of him, too. She turned slightly, and he loosened his hold. For a wild moment she felt like pulling his arms back, so they'd be tightly around her again. She said she was fine, wondering at the strange light in his eyes.

His gaze was riveted on her, and she couldn't look away. Time seemed to stand still, and a smile touched them both. She should move, push away from him, but she didn't think she could make herself. Being in his arms awoke a sensation of safety and protection that she didn't want to give up just yet.

But they couldn't sit on this deserted beach forever, so she dragged her gaze from his and said, "We really should go." Her voice sounded fragile to her ears.

"Yes," he muttered, hastily releasing her.

ॐ

When they touched down at Johnny's field, the last light of day had faded, and flickering lights of the city shimmered in the darkness. Meredith had spent most of the flight keeping her hands from shaking as she worked the control, wondering what had happened back there and what she was going to do about it.

Johnny Westmore got to her as no other man ever had. Being so absorbed with her career, she'd not dated much and didn't quite know what to do around a man, as some girls did. She'd had friendships, but they never seemed to go anywhere, even with Tony, whom she mistakenly had thought cared for her.

She would be much safer to stick to her work and forget Johnny, but she was beginning to doubt that was possible, even if she wanted to. What she wanted was to give in to the urge to spend a lot more time with him and get to know him better. When she finally acknowledged that, she thought, *well, why not? He's not a heartbreaker, and it could be interesting. I might learn about men, so that some day when I'm ready to settle down, I'll know more than I do now.*

She felt proud of herself for this realistic outlook, and she hushed the happy song that sprang to her lips.

Back at the hangar, she took a good look at herself in the bathroom mirror and frowned. She dug through her pockets, looking for her comb to tame the unruly curls springing up around her face. Her eyes were white circles where her goggles had protected her from small flicks of engine oil and dirt.

She rubbed a finger along her eyebrows, looking at herself under lowered lids. Ridiculous. She pursed her lips into a bee-stung pout and whispered to her reflection, "Dahling!" She laughed. Figuring she was not the vamp type, she settled for washing her face and smoothing out her coveralls.

Johnny invited her to dinner, and she agreed, insisting, though, on going home to clean up first. This would be a real date. She ran a bath, sprinkling in a few drops from a small bottle of violet-scented cologne that Aunt Lulu had given her. Resisting the urge to wear her new dress (this was only dinner, after all), she put on a white blouse and her new jumper, and pulled her hair back, fastening it with tortoise shell combs.

When she appeared at the living room doorway, Johnny and Helen's eyes registered their approval. "The little bird has transformed herself into a princess!" said Helen.

Johnny smiled and agreed, his eyes drinking her in. They enjoyed their dinner at a large restaurant near the pier at Ocean Park, and strolled the boardwalk with a hundred other visitors who flocked to the beach.

When he returned her to her door, she shyly held out her hand and thanked him for a lovely evening.

He took her hand and looked deep into her eyes. "My pleasure," he said, almost a murmur.

After a moment of easy silence, she sighed. "Good night,

then."

He let go of her hand and opened the screen door for her. "Need a ride in the morning?"

"I need to work on my routine all morning, getting used to the new engine, so I should leave early."

"How does seven o'clock sound?"

"Fine." It didn't seem like either one of them had moved, but his face was inches from hers. She blinked, then focused her gaze and gently bit her lower lip. His gaze moved back and forth across her face for a long moment.

She stepped back, instantly regretting the action. But the moment was gone. "Good night," she said and slipped inside.

Helen was in bed, and Meredith was glad of the time she'd have alone with her thoughts.

Johnny entered his apartment, feeling as if his world had tilted, but the subtle shift pleased him. He moved to the window and looked out toward the rolling waves. *Is this the good thing I felt was going to happen?* he asked. He heard no answer, but felt a warm glow of approval. *I like her, Lord, I like her very much. But I don't like the way she risks her life for the crowd.* The only sound in his apartment was the ticking of the clock.

I've got to convince her to stop those death-defying stunts, he thought. *But without alienating her.* He got on his knees and talked to God about it.

❧

Meredith practiced all morning, concentrating on getting the feel of the more powerful engine, delighted with the ease with which she did her old stunts, trying out new ones that delighted her even more.

She followed Johnny and Curley over to Meacham's field, and Ernie drove the parts truck.

Both shows were packed, and the stunts went well, except when one of the Spads whirled around and crashed back onto the ground during takeoff, leaving the aviator with a broken arm.

Meredith, Helen, and Johnny turned down an invitation to go to a speakeasy with some of the aviators. Instead, they drove into town and took a streetcar to Pasadena, where they ate a huge Chinese feast in a house-turned-restaurant.

Traffic moved quickly out of town, but Johnny easily kept up with the flow. All three in the front seat, they rode in a festive attitude. "I don't know when I've had so much fun!" said Helen, as Johnny turned the car into their parking area.

"Me, either," he agreed.

At their front door, Helen quickly slipped inside, leaving them alone on the porch.

Meredith edged toward the door, thinking she should go in too, not wanting him to think she was too eager. She glanced up.

His clear blue eyes sparkled back at her. "You look keen tonight," he said, smiling, "to use a current slang word."

She took a quick breath and was about to say thank you, but the words stuck in her throat. She dropped her gaze, wondering what transformation had come over her to make her suddenly shy. Wasn't this good old Johnny? Friend and fellow mechanic? *No, this is much more,* a small voice within seemed to say.

He touched her arm. "Merry?"

She rallied promptly, putting her hand on her arm where he'd touched her. "I'm fine!" she said, her voice a little more brittle than she'd intended.

"I'll pick you up at nine-fifteen tomorrow morning. Bring a Bible," he said. "And whatever you need for the show. We'll go right from church."

She said good night and stepped into the apartment.

Helen came out from the bedroom. "Not much to talk about?"

"Early appointment tomorrow morning. I'm going to church

with him." Meredith pulled out the combs as she passed Helen.

"I told you—he likes you." Helen's voice followed her into the small bathroom. Then Helen stood at the open bathroom door as Meredith washed her hands.

Meredith slowly dried her hands on the worn towel, then folded it back on its rack. "I guess. As a friend."

"He likes *me* as a friend," Helen said. "You, he looks at in a way that is a different kind of like."

In some small, secret part of herself, Meredith enjoyed hearing that. She shrugged. "He can look at me any way he wants," she said, "but it's nothing more than friendship."

Helen turned aside so Meredith could pass her. "You can pretend not to see the sun, but its rays still warm you."

"Is that an old Navajo saying?" Meredith asked, picking up her hairbrush.

Helen laughed. "No, it's something I just made up. But it fits!" She grinned proudly.

"I admit, he's a good man," Meredith agreed, unwilling to say any more.

"You could do a lot worse," said Helen.

Though Meredith tried countless times to get to sleep that night, every time she closed her eyes, Johnny Westmore drifted, uninvited, into her thoughts, settling into her mind and refusing to go away. It troubled her to admit that she couldn't suppress a sharp desire to see him again. The mere thought of the look in his eyes when he caught her fall on the island last night was enough to bring a flash of heat to her cheeks.

What would church would be like? She hadn't been in a church since she came to America. It pained her to think that her mother would have wanted her to attend regularly, but as soon as she was away from her father, she had refused to go anymore.

She finally drifted off into a dreamless, deep sleep. Helen's moving about woke her the next morning. She put on her new

green dress, and though she tried, she couldn't think of any
good reason why she should back out on her promise to go to
church with Johnny.

fourteen

Johnny's eyes almost popped out of his head when she opened the door Sunday morning. The Meredith he'd gotten to know over the past weeks was pretty, but the girl standing before him now was positively gorgeous. "You look beautiful," he said, not shy about complimenting her.

· Blushing, she was grateful when he took her hand and led her to the car. She took a deep breath to steady herself, refusing to be coy and shy around him. She looked boldly at him, enjoying the view. From his pleated tweed trousers to the off-white dress shirt and fawn-colored jacket, he was devastatingly handsome.

After he seated her and got in on his side, he told her that the impossible had happened. "Somebody is taking my ten-year-olds' class this morning," he said, looking over his shoulder to back out of the parking area. "So we'll get to attend the adult class in the main sanctuary."

Meredith's mind went back years to when her father preached at various churches. She and Pearl had a secret sign language to communicate with each other when their interest wandered. She sighed, wondering what Pearl would have looked like and what she'd be doing right now if she'd lived. She'd be twenty-two years old. All Meredith could remember was a frail, imaginative ten-year-old with a beautiful voice.

Fog had rolled in during the night, and Meredith said, "It's sunny a few hundred feet up."

Johnny agreed. Earthbound, they drove with the light flow of traffic going their way, passing crowds going the other way. "Even in the fog, they flock to the beach," he observed.

"At least *we* have a parking space," said Meredith.

"I've had to pull cars out of our lot more than once."

They suddenly passed into sunlight, and the city sparkled ahead. Soon they entered a parking lot lined with palm trees. The Spanish-style white church had a red tile roof with a small, rounded tower with a cross on top.

They went in the side door, and down a few steps. Heavenly smells of freshly baked bread assailed Meredith's senses. Johnny introduced her to a small group of people, and she was warmly welcomed and offered coffee and a cinnamon roll.

He handed her a cup of coffee and said, "The Ladies' League makes these to encourage people to come early to Sunday school."

She breathed in the smell of the warm roll. "Good idea."

They sat at a long dining table, across from a couple in their sixties. People stopped and greeted Johnny and made Meredith so welcome, she began to feel like a visiting celebrity.

After their coffee and roll, they went into the chapel for the class. She had brought her mother's Bible and was satisfied she could still quickly find the references used in the lesson.

The teacher linked an Old Testament passage with a New Testament one, in a way she'd never thought of. The time passed quickly, surprising her that the hour was over so soon. The organist came in and began playing softly, while people arrived, warmly welcoming each other and filling the pews.

Chad slid in beside Meredith, followed by a dark-haired smiling woman in a rose-colored dress, holding the hand of a little girl with brown ringlets. "Miss Bailey!" Chad cried, grinning from ear to ear. He turned to his mom, keeping an eye on Meredith. "Mom! This is the lady I told you about! The one who has her own aeroplane!" He beamed at Meredith.

Johnny reached past Meredith, grabbing his nephew's hand. "Hey there, Tiger. How's school?"

Chad's exuberance waned slightly. "It's okay," he said in a

matter-of-fact tone.

Johnny introduced Meredith to his sister-in-law, their daughter Nell, and his brother Nate, who slid into the seat beside her. The blue-robed choir entered, and the sounds of friendly people greeting one another subsided as the pastor strode onto the platform.

The music touched Meredith the most. She sang the familiar songs, but a sadness crept in as she imagined she heard Pearl singing along. She had to resist the stupid urge to turn around and look for her. She sat quietly through the message, listening to the pastor, unable to shake her feeling of loss and sadness. When they sang the final song, she could barely whisper the words through the ache in her heart.

She was quiet as they said their good-byes to Johnny's family and hurried to the car. She shouldn't have come to church; it only opened old wounds.

"A penny for your thoughts," said Johnny, pulling out onto the busy street.

She bit her lip, looking out her window at the store fronts, fighting hard against her heavy heart that sat like a lead lump in her throat. After a long pause she turned to face him and forced her mouth to curve into a smile. "Oh, nothing important. Just going over my stunts for today." She regretted not being quite truthful, and guiltily, she began to imagine the high wingover.

"So. Did you enjoy church?"

"Yes, very much," she said, thinking of the friendly people and the pastor's message.

Johnny, sensing she was disturbed about something, silently asked God to help her with it and turned the conversation to flying. "I heard there are two guys in Hollywood making a movie, and one of them landed his aeroplane on a moving train. The turbulence whipping up from the cars almost flipped him over."

She told him of one of the aviators in the circus who told her he chased jackrabbits in the desert for excitement.

Thanks to his keeping the subject light, she was able to put her sad memories back where they'd been for the last twelve years.

At the meeting that night, Meacham congratulated the group, making special mention of Meredith's favor with the crowd, promising her a larger place on the handbill. He assured Kate that her latest stunt, dancing the Charleston, was brilliant, and complimented Helen on her originality with the bow and arrow.

Helen left early, to drive to her brother's house, so Johnny took Meredith home. On the way he turned, easing into a smile and said, "Look, a full moon, and it's warm. Let's fly."

She looked at him with surprise. Johnny Westmore had a spontaneous side to him! "Sounds like fun," she said.

Once aloft, he circled his plane over the city lights, dipping his wing near the Richfield Building and the new city hall, flying over darkened groves of trees and fields of various crops. He flew to the coast, swooping over the beaches, then headed east into the desert and landed on a large dry lake.

He cut the engine, and silence engulfed them. He leaned his head back and looked straight up. "Look at the stars, Merry."

She did, staring at them in wonder. Cricket chirps punched the silence.

After a long moment he said, "Let's stretch our legs before we head back."

They climbed out and stood on the white powdery dust. A tumbleweed skittered past them in the light breeze. Tall cacti stood sentinel at the rim of the dry lake, twisting their arms in all directions before the dark backdrop of jagged mountains.

Meredith looked around at the strange landscape lit only by the full moon light. "Where are we?"

"The high desert," he answered. "I like to come here when

the noise and confusion of the city gets to me."

"Does anyone live up here?"

"There are a few communities dotting the area, but nothing like the scramble and fuss in Los Angeles." They walked around the aeroplane, enjoying the peaceful silence. Johnny took off his jacket and spread it on the ground. "Let's sit a while."

They sat, shoulders touching, knees drawn up, and looked toward the mountains. Finally, Johnny spoke. "This morning after church I noticed you were withdrawn, sort of sad. What happened to cause that?"

She was momentarily speechless and glanced away uneasily. "Oh, it was nothing."

"Something bothered you. What was it?"

She picked up a lump of sand and pressed it into grains. "It's not easy to talk about."

"Just tell me what you can."

She studied him. His compelling blue eyes smiled warmly at her. Moonlight washed over his strong face. "Why do you want to know? Is it so important to you?"

Instinctively, he reached out and touched her hand, encouraging her to trust him.

Meredith could feel his concern start to melt the wall around her memories. She wanted more than anything to tell someone all of it and have it changed, made better. But it was too late for that. Pearl was dead. Her mother was dead, and God had sat back and let it happen.

"It's important to me, because I care."

Uneasy under his scrutiny, she looked away.

His soft voice cut through her thoughts. "God cares, too, Merry."

Out of nowhere a wave of anger swept over her. "He does, does He? Did He care about taking the family from a twelve-year-old girl who had no one else? Did He give any reason? Did He need them more than I did?" She leaped up and paced before him. "Did He care enough to offer any comfort?"

Johnny stood before her, and she stopped. He saw pain in her eyes, a pain so deep, so powerful, it hurt him too. "I could give you comfort," he said softly. Her eyes filled with tears. He drew her against him, encouraging her to rest her head on his shoulder. "He cares, Merry. He cares."

Meredith stiffened and moved away from him. She stared at the mountains. His arm lay across her shoulders. "My father was an evangelist," she said. "We traveled all over England when I was young. My sister Pearl was frail from the moment she was born. The midwife didn't think she'd live. But she did. We all doted on her and protected her."

She took a few slow steps, and he walked with her. "She wasn't spoiled, though. We had to take special care, because sometimes it got so cold and damp in the places where we had to stay, she might catch cold. My mother took her twice a year, spring and autumn, to a doctor in London. If there was enough money for my fare, I'd go too."

She stopped, looking at the horizon, visualizing a pain only she could see. "On one trip, when she was ten and I was twelve, I had to stay behind with my father."

She paused, and Johnny moved his hand gently on her shoulder to comfort her.

"The train crashed. A lot of people died. My mother and Pearl never made it to London, and I never saw them again."

She sounded like a mechanical doll, all emotion gone from her voice, either because the memory was too painful to allow feelings, or because she was bravely holding back.

"Once I got past the shock, and the funeral, I tried to find some reason, some logic for it. Why? *Why?* My mother played the piano or organ in my father's services. She taught me my lessons because we were on the road so much I didn't go to school. Pearl was innocent, so sweet. She didn't need to die. I needed her."

"You had your father," his statement was tinged with question.

She glared at him with reproach, as though it was his fault. "My father! He meekly accepted it. 'The Lord giveth, and the Lord taketh away,' he said. And other things like, 'It was meant to be,' 'It was their time.' What baloney! I saw he was unhappy and miserable, but he refused to see their deaths as a horrible, senseless waste of two beautiful people."

"Did you ever forgive him?"

"Why should I?" She felt a nauseating, sinking feeling of wretchedness. "I wish—"

"What do you wish?"

"I wish it'd been me, instead of Mama and Pearl on that train. They could have coped with losing me a lot better than I did with losing them."

"How can you say that?" He held her by her shoulders, his eyes brimming with tenderness.

"I was a good child, but after the accident, I was never able to be anything but trouble to my father. Death would have been easier than living every day with the thoughts I had every time I closed my eyes."

"And you think God doesn't care?"

"I know He doesn't."

"What do you think He should have done for you?"

She felt desolate and assailed by bitterness. "I don't know! He's God! He could have done *something*!"

Angry tears trembled on her eyelids. Johnny tried to think of an answer that wouldn't sound like a cliché, while she challenged him with her hurt, angry look. Still holding her shoulders, he stepped closer, looking directly into her eyes. "I don't know the whole story, but I do know God, and I'm absolutely certain that He cares and will comfort you if you'll let Him."

Meredith shook her head, confused and torn by conflicting emotions. "You don't understand!" She pulled away from him and walked a few feet away. She stood, arms crossed, fighting back tears. She could barely hold onto her thoughts while she was so close to him, but now that a small distance separated them, the injustice of her mother's and sister's deaths came back into focus. She turned and looked at him across the desert night. "As soon as I was old enough, I got away and never went back into a church again."

"Until today."

"It's been seven years."

He closed the gap between them, standing before her. "You're angry that God didn't do something you expected. But you do believe in Him."

She was more shaken than she cared to admit, both by bringing all this up again and by his gentle concern. "I can't deny there is a God; I feel Him when I'm flying. But that's the only place I sense His presence. Not in church."

"Then why were you upset this morning?"

"What's the point?" She shook her head. "I don't know!" She walked past him toward the plane. "Just leave it, okay? I told you more than I should have. Forget it."

"I won't forget, and you didn't tell me anything you shouldn't have. I said, I care."

She climbed into the plane, then scrambled back out. "I'll crank the prop."

They flew back over the hills. Johnny looked at the back of her head, held high in the seat before him, and thought about what she'd said. His lips thinned with anger. *She's believed a lie all these years. A lie from the pit of hell, that kept her from the peace and joy of trusting God.* The throbbing of the engine covered his muttered prayer for God to show Himself to her, for Him to let her know how much He really cared for her.

They landed, tucked the plane in for the night, and drove home, both silent with their own thoughts.

❧

For the next two weeks, neither talked about that night, except for Johnny on his knees, talking to God about it. They were friendly as they went about their routines, Johnny with his expanding business and his repair shop, Meredith with her aeroplane, practicing her stunts, creating new ones, and taking Helen up for lessons.

She and Helen cooked dinner for Johnny one night, and he took her out to eat after work a couple of times. They took companionable walks along the beach and talked of everything but the serious issues she'd brought up that night in the desert. Johnny seemed to simply enjoy her company.

One evening he didn't get back before she left, and she realized that she looked forward to seeing him every day more than she cared to admit. Every night he sneaked into her thoughts just before she went to sleep.

She couldn't keep from pondering what he'd said to her out on the desert. Mostly she thought about his simple question, did she forgive her father? Of course she was angry at her father. What did that have to do with God's failure to stop the accident? She forced her mind away from that subject, which was very close to the possibility that she might also be mad at God.

She tossed and turned, trying to deal with the crazy thoughts in her head, finally getting up without waking Helen and going to the living room. She pulled the curtain back and looked out. The setting moon left a silver ribbon reaching toward her across the waves.

She could see no way to deal with the problem, except by doing what she'd always done—living her life, not thinking about what was past and gone. She tiptoed back to the bedroom and climbed under her covers, resolving to live her life as usual—no past, just the future. It always worked before, and she was certain it would now.

&

That Sunday evening Jim Meacham announced that Bradley's Madly Daring Flying Show which garnered thousands of fans in San Diego, was coming to Los Angeles. He said that hordes of people had begged him to bring his Circus to San Francisco, so rather than face Bradley's competition here in L.A., moving to San Francisco was his plan. "This being Thanksgiving weekend," he said, "we'll have three final days: Friday, Saturday, and Sunday, with a spectacular dusk-to-dark finale each day, with sparklers and lights. December fifth we'll be in San Francisco!"

The group was stunned for a minute, then excited. Meredith, Helen, and Johnny looked at each other, weighing questions about the move. Someone called out, "Where in San Francisco?" Another asked, "When do you want us there?" Other questions followed.

Meredith and Helen rode home with Johnny. Helen said, "I can't go. It's too far from my brother and my family."

"What will you do?" asked Meredith, knowing Helen needed the money from the show.

She stared straight ahead at the windshield. "I don't know. Maybe Bradley's Mad bunch could use an Indian maiden."

Johnny looked over at Meredith. "What about you?"

"I don't know," she said, wondering if this could be the answer to her dilemma about forgetting the past and going forward. The thought of leaving and the knowledge that she'd miss Johnny caused a small pain in her heart, but she gritted her teeth and told herself that was precisely why she should go. She was getting too attached here.

On the other hand, her savings were built up to a point where she was almost ready to start negotiations for hangar space for her school. Maybe now was the time to do it. The good feelings that accompanied those thoughts worried her. Was she just rationalizing so she could be close to Johnny? He and Helen were the closest friends she'd had since Pearl died.

She pondered the idea of going to San Francisco, counted her money, including the large amount she'd receive for nine shows this weekend, and tried to keep strictly to impersonal, financial reasons. She had to keep friendship separate from business. Her goal of having a school was all that needed to be considered. Was this move good for that goal or not?

※

On Wednesday night, Johnny's brother and his family stopped by the hangar. Chad ran in and almost knocked Meredith over. "'Scuse me," he said breathlessly. "Is Uncle Johnny here?"

Meredith looked out under the hangar door rail. "He's up there, but he'll be down in a minute."

Chad's father came in behind him. He looked a lot like an older version of Johnny, only his shoulders weren't quite as broad, and his hair curled slightly, where Johnny's was straight. He smiled and held out his hand to her. "Nice to see you again."

"Nice to see you, too," she answered.

"We've been out shopping for last minute things for Thanksgiving Dinner tomorrow and were in the neighborhood."

"Can Miss Bailey come to dinner, Dad, can she?" Chad pulled on his father's hand and looked imploringly up into his face.

Nate smiled down at him. "Of course." He looked at Meredith. "We have plenty, and we'd love to have you."

Meredith hesitated. "No, I can't . . . I, um—"

"Please!" begged Chad. "You can see my dog Ace!"

His father put a hand on the boy's shoulder. "Maybe she has other plans." He gave Meredith a questioning look.

"No, but . . ." Johnny's plane touched down on the airstrip behind Nate.

"Hooray! Then you'll come!" Chad clapped his hands. "I'm going to tell Mom." He ran out of the hangar.

Nate watched the boy fondly, then turned to Meredith. "He's a bit rambunctious, but we'd be honored if you'd join us."

Meredith said, "Thank you. I'll come."

Johnny turned off his engine, and Chad ran to meet him. "Miss Bailey's coming to Thanksgiving dinner!"

Johnny's eyes met Meredith's over the boy's head. "That's good!" he said.

Meredith's heart turned over in response, and in that instant she knew. She had to leave. She was going to San Francisco with Meacham's Circus.

fifteen

Johnny climbed out of the cockpit and grinned at Chad, whose joy at Meredith's coming to dinner matched his own. He put an affectionate arm around the boy's shoulder and glanced at her. Her green eyes smoldered with a faraway intensity that sent him a message he couldn't decipher.

Edith was out of the car, Emily in her arms, five-year-old Nell holding her hand. "The whole family!" he observed. "To what do I owe this honor?"

"Last minute shopping for tomorrow," she said. Johnny knelt down to properly greet Nell, who shyly smiled at him. Chad proudly announced that Meredith was coming to Thanksgiving dinner, and Edith's smile broadened in approval.

Beginning to feel a bit overwhelmed by all this family togetherness, Meredith nodded her thanks for the invitation and went back to work. There were so many things to think about, now that she'd made her decision to leave with the circus. She felt good to be back on track to her goal toward total independence.

On the way home Johnny happily talked about his family and the loads of food that would be cooked. She half listened, wondering if he was exaggerating for her benefit. Well, tomorrow she'd see. This would be her last week here, and she might never see Johnny Westmore again. She intended to enjoy the time, so she'd have a memory that would have to last a lifetime.

Early the next morning they drove to the hangar, to take two college-aged boys on a two-hour flight to Fresno. Johnny flew them all comfortably, including Meredith, in his modified Standard.

On the way back, flying over the mountains, Meredith was busily forming questions. She saw how using the aeroplane for transport could be financially beneficial. How did he get passengers? How much profit was there over the cost of gas, oil, and other necessities? What about packages? She'd design a holder and cover for Birdie's front cockpit to ferry boxes from one point to another. This could be a sideline which might even support her school while it was starting up.

They flew over the San Fernando Valley to an airport near his brother's home in Burbank. Nate and an older woman were there to meet them. Meredith ran her fingers through her unruly curls and confidently walked beside Johnny.

He gave the older woman a big hug, then introduced her as his mother. She was about the same height as Meredith, with grey-streaked blonde hair. Meredith could see that Nate and Johnny got their height from their father.

"Call me Sarah," she said, smiling and offering her hand to Meredith. Driving from the air field, Sarah Westmore commented that when they'd first come to Burbank, it was an agricultural area. "Now look at it!" she exclaimed, pointing to signs proclaiming new subdivisions of homes.

"Everyone wants to live here!" said Nate.

When they arrived at the house, they were met by the children and Edith, who came out carrying a dishtowel. Meredith was swept along into the house, which smelled deliciously of turkey, spices, and promises of a great feast.

Chad took them outside to see Ace. Johnny picked up the fat puppy and asked, "What are you feeding him? Tiger food? He's twice as big!" He put the squirming pup down. "Wiggles as much as ever, I see. Should've called him Wiggly."

Chad's mother called him, and Johnny took Meredith on a walk through the plum orchard. "Since my father died, Mom gets lonely. She loves these family get-togethers. I'm glad you're here." He took her hand.

His gaze roved over her quickly, as she walked beside him in her blue jumper and white blouse. She was petite enough to be delicate, even fragile, until one saw the animated fire shining in her eyes and the obstinate red-gold curls that refused to be tamed.

Meredith breathed in the scent of trees and the dusty lanes. The quiet was broken by the calling of birds. She marveled at how warm the air was for November. What would life be like if she lived like this? She drew her lips in thoughtfully for a moment, then sighed and looked up between the leafy branches to the sky where she belonged.

A husband and wife and ten-year-old daughter had joined the Thanksgiving gathering while Meredith and Johnny were in the orchard. They'd come to sunny California to start their new life and had met the Westmores at church.

Soon they all gathered around the table. Beaming proudly, Edith brought out an enormous, beautifully browned turkey and set it before Nate. They all murmured compliments, and Johnny held the chair for his mother. When she was seated, they all sat, except Emily who was already in her high chair. A lace tablecloth covered the large well-worn mahogany table. Nate clinked his knife against his water glass, signaling for quiet.

When their happy chatter ceased, he bowed his head, and they did the same. "Lord, we thank You for the bountiful feast set before us, and for the friends and family gathered here to-day."

His prayer reminded Meredith of her father praying at one of her birthday dinners. They, too, had always had guests around the table.

Everyone echoed Nate's "Amen," and the happy chatter resumed as food was passed and spooned onto their plates. She smiled back at the happy faces around the table and felt a curious sense of belonging. Johnny laughed at something Chad said, then glanced at Meredith, his grin flashing briefly.

The group around the table discussed all the things they had to thank God for. Chad got everyone's attention saying, "Nell was really sick last year, but God made her better!" Nell nodded her head, and everyone happily agreed that God was good, indeed.

For some reason Chad asked, "Do you believe in God, Miss Bailey?"

Meredith hesitated, feeling a gamut of conflicting emotions. She looked around the table. Eager faces smiled at her, expecting her to say yes. After all, she thought, she'd accepted Christ when she was very young. She glanced at Johnny. The look on his face mingled confidence and tenderness. "I've been a Christian ever since I can remember," she said to Chad.

Johnny reached out and took her hand beneath the table. She snatched it away as if she'd been stung. She refused to look at him and was quiet through the rest of dinner and dessert. Edith thanked her for offering to help wash dishes, but she said there were too many women in the kitchen.

Desperately needing to be alone, Meredith slipped out of the kitchen to the back porch. The sunset over the orchard shot brilliant streaks of gold and orange across the sky. She stepped out into the night and wandered restlessly down the wooden steps.

She walked down the walk, past well-tended primroses, left the yard, and meandered through the trees. She leaned against the smooth trunk of one and let the confused thoughts tumble through her. She'd told Chad she was a Christian. She'd been in enough church services and Sunday schools to know exactly what that meant.

Saying it, putting it into words, somehow brought a whole flood of impressions and thoughts rushing forward from the past. Bible verses, action songs she and Pearl learned, the excitement of going to new places, the feeling of God always beside her, and much, much more.

All the memories and feelings felt as though they had been held back by a long piece of rubber, and when she claimed to be a Christian, they all snapped back and hit her fully between her eyes. She realized that God hadn't changed, and if she wasn't walking with Him now, that wasn't because of Him—so it must be because of her.

At first she was angry that she'd let herself be drawn into this obviously religious family, but then she realized her problems weren't really their fault. She'd been graciously welcomed and treated with kindness. No, this was something within herself that she had to deal with.

She heard footsteps, and forcing these thoughts from her mind, she focused on the present. It was time to go home.

Nate and Nell appeared, and he remarked on the lovely evening. She agreed and went inside to find Johnny.

He had wondered where Meredith disappeared after dinner. He'd started out the back porch to find her, but Chad was there, feeding Ace. He convinced Johnny to come back inside and read the children a story from his favorite book.

Meredith came back about halfway through the story, seeming distracted and quiet. Chad scooted over to make room for her on the floor, and she sat beside him.

Holidays, since her mother and Pearl died, had been lonely, silent occasions. Her father hadn't the heart to try, and when she left home, she didn't bother. Now she sensed she'd needed this all these years, not even knowing it was missing. She forced herself to listen to the story Johnny was reading and pushed the disturbing thoughts away.

In the plane flying home, Meredith tried to think of a way to tell him she was leaving. They were such good friends, and she'd miss him. She'd miss Helen, too, she reminded herself. But that wasn't the same. She detoured her thoughts again, wondering if there was anything safe to think of anymore. *Think of San Francisco,* she told herself, trying to remember everything she'd heard about the City by the Bay.

Driving home from the hangar, she kept the topic on the afternoon at Nate and Edith's. The sidewalks were filled with people strolling after dinner, and traffic was heavy. Johnny asked, "Are you thirsty? We could stop for a Coke."

"Thanks, but I have a lot to do. I need to get home as soon as possible."

He glanced at her. "Are you okay?"

"I'm fine," she said, then pressed her lips shut and looked straight ahead.

Johnny knew better than to annoy her by pressing for an answer, but he said, "I know Chad put you on the spot back there, but you handled it well."

She was amazed that he mentioned that, as if he knew what she was thinking.

When she didn't answer, he wondered if her mood had anything to do with their conversation in the desert. Maybe she was rethinking her beliefs. She certainly was deep in thought about something.

Meredith clenched her jaw, refusing to be distracted by his charm. She had to concentrate on the only thing that worked when emotions threatened to overrun her cool determination. Flying. Her school. She forced herself to imagine being at Birdie's controls. *Smell the gasoline and oil. Feel the engine vibrate as you rumble over the ground. Feed more power to the engine. Look out over the wing, through the wires and struts. Feel the vibrations fade and disappear in that breathless moment when the wheels lift off the ground.*

She felt secure in these familiar thoughts. This was the reality of her life. This was all she had to depend on. She was glad she'd made the decision to leave. Concentrating on her goal would be easier now.

Johnny turned the corner to their street and glanced at her.

She sat, serenely wrapped in her own thoughts. Her hair glistened in the shadows, small curls twisted across her forehead and down the side of her neck. She felt so right, here beside him. At that moment he realized that she'd crept into his heart and become very dear to him. *When did it happen?* he wondered.

The car stopped. Meredith looked up at him with an inner fire still glowing in her eyes from her mental pictures. "Oh! We're here!" she said.

"You seemed to be miles away," Johnny said, and turning toward her, he stretched his long legs out and draped his arm across the steering wheel.

In the friendly silence she clasped her hands beneath her chin and looked out at the stars. "Yes, miles away." She suddenly dropped her hands, reached for the door handle, and looked back at him. "Thanks for today. I enjoyed it very much."

He leaped out and ran to her side, but she was already out and closing her door. He took her elbow as she quickly walked to her door.

"Helen is here," she said, seeing the light inside. "But she forgot to turn on the porch light."

Johnny hesitated a moment, his eyes on her lovely profile. Then he tenderly slid his hand from her elbow up to her shoulder and turned her to face him. A sweet pink rush tinted her cheeks and made her eyes glitter as her gaze locked with his.

He swallowed tightly as his large hand gently held her face. She looked up at him, and he did what seemed the most natural thing in the world to do. He closed the short gap between them and gently kissed her.

Though the kiss was tender and brief, Meredith's mouth tingled, and all she could think of was that she wanted him to kiss her again.

No! Wake up! she thought wildly. In the space of a couple of seconds she'd forgotten all about flying and her school.

Abruptly, she pulled away from him and opened the door. "Good night," she said, and hurried inside, as if she were fleeing from danger.

Johnny watched her go, unable to relate her skittish attitude with the softness she'd shown seconds ago. The moment seemed perfect, and his heart and soul were drawn to her. He shook his head, wondering if he should have gone more slowly. After all, she hadn't consented yet to give up her wildly dangerous occupation. He headed toward his apartment, his breathing ragged.

He stopped at his door, turned and looked back for a moment, then walked onto the boardwalk and down to the beach to think.

Her lips still tingling from his kiss, Meredith glanced through the curtains as Johnny walked away.

Helen came out from the hallway. She pulled a brush through her long black hair. "Did you have a nice time?"

"Yes." Meredith touched her fingertips to her lips and allowed herself a moment to muse on her first real kiss. She'd always been too busy to get romantically close to a man. Tony had kissed her, but that didn't count, because all the time she was pulling away from him.

Helen tossed her dark mane behind her and said, "Come have a cup of coffee. We've been going seven days a week, and this would be a good time to stop and talk."

Meredith was glad for the chance to spend time with Helen. That would help her get her mind off Johnny. She followed her into the kitchen, and got the cups while Helen filled the percolator.

Helen told of her day with her brother and family, and Meredith talked of the Westmore clan's feast. She was thinking tonight would be a good time to tell Helen she was leaving, when Helen herself brought up the subject.

"I've decided to talk to Bradley, about being in his show. My stunts are unique enough that he'll hire me." She sipped her coffee. "What about you?"

"I'm going with Meacham," said Meredith.

Helen set her cup down carefully. "I thought you might. I'll miss you. Keep in touch."

"I'll miss you, too," Meredith told her, wondering how she'd gotten so attached to Venice and Los Angeles in so short a time.

"How did Johnny take the news?"

"I haven't told him yet." She shrugged one shoulder. "There's really nothing between us, so it won't matter."

"Right." Helen didn't look at all convinced.

For some reason Meredith didn't want her to think she was a coward. "Look, I know he's a nice guy and handsome as they come, but I have my future all planned out, and it'll be years before there'll be room for a man."

"Do you think he'd slow you down?"

She gazed at Helen. "He's a traditional kind of guy, a family man. You know—the little cottage with a white picket fence, wife in the kitchen, babies, and all that."

"Did he tell you that?" Helen leaned forward, her dark eyes smoldering with interest.

"No, but I can't see myself in that role. I don't . . ."

"You don't want to get hurt?" Meredith warmed her hands on the hot cup and didn't answer. "No one wants to get hurt. Not even Johnny," said Helen.

Meredith reached out to her. "I have a life, and a career to concentrate on now, and I've got to be about it."

"I understand, Little Sister. But when you find the right man, all that won't be as important to you."

"Well, Johnny Westmore isn't that man."

"Right." Helen smiled at her with that unconvinced look.

ಜ

The next three days were a whirlwind of activity, flying the two regular shows, and an after-dusk show with sparklers, flood lights, and small lights strung around the field. Meredith attached sacks of flour on the end of each wing, and pulled a trip-wire which punched a hole, spewing out flour while she wrote a big "M" in the sky. The lights picked it up beautifully, and the crowd loved it.

She kept busy, avoiding Johnny as much as possible, and when they were together, she kept the conversation light.

Sunday night after the last show, he walked over to talk with her. He knew she was keyed up about the nine shows they'd done this weekend, but he didn't like being avoided.

She was standing with Helen and Joe, smiling at something one of them had said, when Joe beckoned him to join them. Meredith's glowing green eyes met his, and the familiar force arched between them. She lowered her lashes and looked aside.

Joe raised an eyebrow. "Well, this stint is over. Maybe you'll be supplying parts and service for Bradley's planes."

"Maybe." He moved between Helen and Meredith, standing close to her. "Let's celebrate the ending of one era and the beginning of another."

Meredith's breath caught in her throat. She should have told him she was leaving. With an ease she didn't feel, she said, "I have to go to the mansion." She lifted a hand and stepped out of the circle. "Bye."

Johnny reached out and took her hand. "What do you mean, go to the mansion? The meeting tonight is for those who are going to San Francisco." His eyes searched her face, seeking answers.

She kept her voice free of expression. "I know."

Helen spoke up, saying, "I'll see you later, Merry. Come on, Joe. Let's check some braces."

Johnny tightened his grip on her hand and led her away from the hangars. "Are you going to San Francisco?" he asked quietly.

"Yes," she said, turning away from him.

"What's there, that you can't get here?"

"Nothing," she admitted, thinking that what was between them would have to be just that—nothing. "Nothing but working to save up for my flying school and a hangar to put it in."

"If it's only money, stay here and work with me. You're an excellent mechanic, and I could do twice as many deliveries with another aeroplane."

She closed her eyes. A pang of pain seeped into her breast. "Johnny, thank you for the offer, but I need to do this myself."

"I'm not offering charity, Meredith." He planted his hands on his hips in agitation. "I'm offering work."

"I appreciate that. But I'm going to San Francisco." It was the hardest thing she'd ever done, to smile up at him and see the play of emotions on his face as he realized she wasn't going to stay.

He shook his head in disbelief. "There's more than one way to get money. You'd rather risk your life, to satisfy some female urge to be independent and show everyone you can do it all by yourself."

She felt anger, like a red shadow, rise in her. She refused to be vulnerable to him. "I can, and I will do it all by myself," she said, glaring at him.

"Independence has its price, Merry. Some day you'll find it's not pleasant to be alone. And you'll be alone if you shut out your friends." That she could leave so easily hurt him.

"I don't need friends." She started to walk away.

"You will, and when you do, give me a call."

Her feet stopped in midstride, and she looked back at him. He held his head high, standing tall and straight, gazing at her with a bleak, tight-lipped smile on his face. "Thank you for that. Good-bye, Johnny," she said in a shaky voice, then forced herself to walk away from him.

"God goes with you," he called after her. "He's always there for you."

She kept on walking, and thought, *I wish I could believe that.*

sixteen

Meredith packed up her things the next day. There was no reason to stay in Los Angeles any longer than necessary.

She and Helen had lunch together for the last time, then Helen took her to Johnny's hangar. Meredith gave her a big hug and fought off tears.

"Keep in touch," said Helen.

"I will," she agreed, determining to correspond with this new friend. Perhaps Johnny was partly right about friends. She did feel good to have a comrade to keep in touch with.

She said good-bye to Ernie and assured Curley she hoped to return to open her flying school in Los Angeles. "Too bad Johnny's not here to say good-bye, too," he said. She told him she'd already said her good-byes to Johnny.

Standing in the step built into Birdie's side, she took her basket, suitcase, and tool chest as Curley handed them to her. She loaded them into the front cockpit. He turned her prop, and she took off, waving a last good-bye to the three of them.

She flew up through the valley, stopping twice to refuel and check Birdie over. She was delighted that her new engine got her to San Francisco in less time than the old OX-5 would have.

She landed in the late afternoon at a good-sized air strip a few miles south of the city. A crowd had gathered to see Meacham's fighter planes that had arrived before her. Several spectators ran to meet her when she taxied up beside them.

She found an inexpensive room in a boardinghouse near the air field. Although she was glad to see the other aviators and other friendly faces, she spent most of her time practicing and visiting airfields in the area, learning all she could about new aeroplanes she hadn't seen before.

The second week of the show Meacham offered her the chance to perform a new stunt, flying over a speeding boat and picking up a wing walker with a rope hanging from her wheel brace. She practiced the stunt, but she found she no longer felt a sense of challenge.

The excitement was gone, and she felt oddly restless, even a little bored. After the first weekend of successful shows, she stood on the grass behind the boardinghouse. The day had been beautiful. Sunny and warm, with afternoon fog seeping over the hills behind her. Water in the bay moved in choppy restlessness as she looked out over it, thinking maybe it was time to give up stunt flying and start her flying school.

She inhaled the damp air and wished she'd worn her sweater. Sounds of music and conversation drifted out from the house's windows. She'd earned more money to add to her savings, and she was happy. She frowned to herself, admitting that maybe she wasn't happy, but at least she could say she was content.

She missed her friends in Los Angeles, though. Did Helen like working for Bradley? How was Johnny doing? Did he get the U.S. Mail contract? Did he get the commercial sidecar he'd wanted for his motorcycle? What was he doing this minute?

She sighed as an aeroplane made its approach to land nearby. It looked like Johnny's Standard. She felt an unfamiliar sense of loss that became a heavy feeling in her heart.

She fought down a suffocating knot in her throat and went inside to the living room where other guests sat listening to the radio. Still fighting off sadness, she picked up a magazine and started to read. Finally, she gave up and went to her room.

She sat on the edge of her bed, clasping her hands in her lap, then, in frustration got up to walk from the door to the window, the only space in the small room. Loneliness wasn't new to her; she'd dealt with it for years, pushing it away to strive for her goal. Now, it would not be pushed aside.

She wondered if withdrawing from social activities had been wise. Perhaps she should socialize more with the aviators. They made it plain that they'd enjoy her company, especially one handsome veteran. No, that wasn't the answer.

She sat back on the bed, then laid back on the pillow, her hands beneath her head. The last thing Johnny said to her was that God was always with her. Did he mean it in the sense that God was everywhere, therefore by default, with her? *No,* she thought, *he seemed to mean it in a personal way.*

Bible verses she and Pearl had learned floated through her mind. *"I will never leave you nor forsake you,"* and *"Neither height, nor depth, nor angels, nor. . . ."* She couldn't think of the whole list of things that could not separate her from the love of God.

Other verses came to her, and the feeling of loneliness left. She couldn't stop the hot tears that welled up and spilled from her eyes. She wiped them away and abruptly sat up. *What is happening to me?* She paced the room again in agitation. Johnny must have touched something inside that brought up old memories, old Bible verses, and an old life that she'd walked away from years ago. That life hadn't worked then and certainly wouldn't work now.

To get her mind off Johnny, God, and emotionally upsetting subjects, she picked up her writing tablet and a pen, and began a letter to her Aunt Lulu.

❧

Returning from the Federal Building to the air field in San Diego, Johnny walked along the sidewalk beneath brightly strung Christmas decorations. He was glad he was busy and his business growing. But even though the pace was getting hectic, and he was seriously thinking of hiring another mechanic, he could hardly keep his mind on his work.

All he could think of was Meredith, the way she looked as

she said her last good-bye the day she walked away from him. He couldn't close his eyes at night without his head filling with thoughts of her. The wind blowing her hair as she called to the seal at Catalina Island, the laughter in her eyes when they drove up Mulhullond Drive for their picnic, how eagerly she worked to install the new Hisso engine, the look in her eyes the night he kissed her . . .

The feeling of rightness, of absolute certainty that in his arms was where she belonged, preyed on his mind. How was he going to spend the rest of his life without her?

Without her? He rejected that thought. It was unthinkable. But what could he do? She went her own way and had been gone three weeks without a call or a note to either him or Helen. If they mattered to her, she would have at least made contact.

He checked in with Adam Shelton and told him he'd accepted an offer from the Post Office for a same-day mail run from San Diego to Santa Barbara. Shelton congratulated him, and Johnny told him that letters or packages to deliver would be brought to the air field before noon.

On the way back to Los Angeles, the drone of the engine faded into the background as his thoughts turned to Meredith. He wondered what she would be doing for Christmas. He'd be with his family, yet he'd be alone. Empty days stretched out before him, followed by lonely nights.

"God," he said aloud, his voice lost in the engine's throbbing, "I miss her. At first I didn't think she was what I wanted, because of her crazy flying stunts, but I can't get her out of my mind. I love her." He looked to the left at a large steamer coming to shore, as he pondered on what he'd just said.

He was used to voicing his most personal thoughts with God, but he wasn't sure if the admission that he loved her was a confession of weakness or the embracing of a wondrous truth.

"God, remember when You seemed to be telling me something wonderful was about to happen? Was it Meredith coming into my life?" He looked ahead through the whirling propeller and waited for some response, but all he got was an all-over good feeling that God was smiling down on him.

"Is she the one?" he repeated. Again, joy washed all over him so that he felt like laughing. He seemed to see her face, smiling at him.

He thought about this for a few moments, then said, "I take that to mean yes." But convincing her seemed more difficult than trying to fly backwards. He decided that after Christmas he'd go to San Francisco and see her. Maybe he'd even take Helen, to ensure a warm reception. *Coward,* he told himself.

❧

Christmas was on a Thursday, and he delivered a present to Helen on his way to his brother's home. She hadn't heard from Meredith personally, but an aviator told her that Meredith was doing well, and the crowds loved her and her purple aeroplane. Johnny told Helen he was going up after the holidays and invited her to go along. She grinned and said she'd think about it.

He didn't have to wait, because early Saturday morning, the twenty-seventh, he got an urgent phone call from Meacham. "Westmore! One of our Spads had an accident. Ruined the prop. The only one available around here is as flimsy as a toothpick. Get one here before noon, and I'll pay double for it, plus your expenses."

"I'll get on it right away." He got directions, dressed quickly, and sped on his motorcycle to the hangar. He hefted the heavy propeller into his DeHaviland and took off within forty minutes from Meacham's call.

As he neared San Francisco, a warm glow of anticipation made him eager to get there. He reminded himself that Meredith might not be as thrilled to see him as he was about seeing her. He decided the best course of action would be to watch her perform, then approach her after the show.

The moment he landed, Meacham and one of the aviators ran out to meet him, pointing to the row of hangars, shouting that the Spad was around back. He saw Meredith's purple Jenny, and a smile overtook him.

"Thanks for coming," said Meacham. "Can you stay for the show? I'll settle with you then."

"I'll stay." Johnny and the aviator went right to work and installed the new propeller.

He carried his toolbox to the hangar, in case he was needed there. Many of the aviators greeted him, shaking his hand and welcoming him to the Bay area. The show began, and he stood in the shadows observing. He was amazed by how easily his eyes were drawn to one small unruly-haired, animated miss.

He watched proudly as she expertly guided her craft into the air, but he couldn't keep from wincing at her spiraling, looping aerobatics overhead. Sam worked the crowd well, having them alternately cheering and gasping in fright. Johnny stared in shock, as a motorboat cruised close to shore, and Sam announced that she would fly closely over the boat, so that a fearless hero, defying death, could grab a rope hanging from the aeroplane and be lifted into the air.

The motorboat had gone a few hundred yards down the coast, then turned and suddenly began gaining speed. Meredith zoomed behind it, catching up, and dropped the ladder. Just as they were in front of the crowd, she was directly over the boat, matching speed for speed. The stunt man stood on the back of the boat, looking over his shoulder, watching her approach.

Johnny held his breath, knowing she was dangerously close to the speed at which Jennies tend to stall. The crowd was hushed. The only sounds were the aeroplane and motorboat engines in a growling duet.

He grimaced as Meredith's propellers whirled dangerously close to the idiot standing on the boat, but they passed over him, and he reached up for the rope ladder dangling from the bar between the wheels. He missed the center, grabbing instead the side of the rope with one hand.

The plane lifted him off the boat, swinging crazily with one arm, clawing for the rung with the other. Women in the crowd screamed, and all eyes watched, fascinated, as the man managed to grab the wheel, setting the plane slightly off balance.

Meredith fought to keep the wings level, wondering what could have gone wrong. She lifted her right wing to compensate for the extra weight on that side, when suddenly the weight wasn't there any more, and she veered crazily to the left as the stunt man fell into the water.

She maneuvered the rudder and ailerons to straighten out and climb back into the air. But she felt the sickening bump of her plane hitting something. Fear, black and heavy, swept through her as she fought to keep control. Then, as if guided by an invisible hand, the plane straightened itself, and Meredith nosed it up into the air. She wondered what she had hit and what the damage was. Maybe the tail skid had hit the mast of a sailboat. When she stabilized, she'd lean out and try to assess the damage.

Johnny watched in horror as Meredith fought to stay steady as the man beneath her grabbed the wheel, then let go and dropped into the Bay. The sudden shift of weight caused her to swing to the left, almost cartwheeling into the docks. Instead, she grazed her left wheel on a dock piling, knocking it loose and leaving it dragging at an angle.

Reaching into his toolbox, he hastily retrieved his tool bag and ran onto the field where the next aviator sat in his Sopwith Pup, ready to start his stunts. "She needs help. Take me up!" He climbed onto the wing, standing close to the cockpit, looping his right arm over the wing brace. He handed the bag to the aviator who scooted over as far as the control stick would allow and stuffed the bag on beside him.

They took off in a hurry. Johnny shouted to the aviator to get as close as he could, then maneuver beneath her so he could fix the wheel.

The aviator nodded and flew toward Meredith's plane. Johnny could hardly keep his eyes open in the gale force wind that threatened to tear him loose from his precarious moorings and fling him backward into space. Only his determination to save her, and a quick prayer, kept his arm locked around the brace as they climbed.

They flew near Meredith, and she looked over at them. Behind her goggles her eyes were round with alarm. He motioned for her to fly level and steady, then he leaned into the cockpit and clumsily opened his tool bag and retrieved a Ford wrench, screwdriver, and a small roll of wire.

He turned his head from the direct blast of wind from the prop wash and pulled himself onto the fuselage in front of the aviator, thankful for the hole in the top wing where the machine gun used to be. He wedged his arms and shoulders through, standing in the heavy wind. He glanced back at the aviator, who was looking up at the underside of Meredith's plane, positioning Johnny just beneath her left wheel.

Knowing he had less than a minute to perform a miracle, he assessed the problem, reached up, and deftly twisted the outer axle pin and adjusted the wheel clamp. He tightened one of the spoke fasteners and spun the wheel with his left hand. It turned correctly, and he let out a deep breath, which was snatched away by the wind.

He dropped his arms, which suddenly ached from the effort of holding them steadily above his head against the wind. They dropped from Meredith's plane and peeled off to their left.

A speck of something flew into Johnny's right eye, and he closed both in pain. He rubbed his eye and fought to open them. Lowering himself, he scraped his side on the gun mount as he slid down the fuselage, feeling for the lower wing with his feet.

His left foot touched the wing, and he reached for the front brace to steady himself. A gust of wind blasting out of nowhere knocked his hand aside, and he stumbled and fell, hitting his head against something sharp protruding from behind the fire wall. He slid sideways along the wing, frantically grabbing for a hold. The Sopwith didn't have as many criss-crossed wires as a Jenny did, and there was little to grab. The wind slammed him up against the strut and he grasped it with all his strength before he blacked out.

The aviator skillfully flew so that Johnny would not be shifted from his pinned-down position between the outer struts. Very carefully, the aviator came in and did the softest landing he'd ever done. Nevertheless, the aeroplane bounced somewhat as he taxied over the grassy field.

The crowd cheered the amazing rescue, not realizing Johnny's injuries. The jarring of the landing knocked him loose, and he slid from the wing to the ground. The crowd uttered a shocked "Oh!" as an ambulance sped toward him.

Meredith came in behind the Sopwith, fighting to keep Birdie from twisting to the right but managing to land safely. She leaped out and ran to the ambulance where attendants were placing Johnny inside.

She approached with dread. He looked so very limp. "Is he alive?" Just thinking of the alternative tore at her insides.

"He's alive," assured the attendant, closing the door. They roared off with a cloud of dust, leaving her looking wildly about.

The Sopwith aviator put his hand on her shoulder. "He'll make it. He's the bravest man I've ever seen! He's tough."

Jim Meacham, who was also there, agreed. "He's one in a million."

"Where are they taking him?" Meredith tried to keep control of her voice, but she felt like screaming.

Meacham walked toward the hangars with her. "He'll be at Mercy Hospital. I know you're his friend. I'll get someone to pull your aeroplane off the field and take you there."

Meredith glanced back at Birdie, leaning slightly to her left behind the Sopwith. "Tell them to be careful," she said, following him into the hangar, where Tim and Slim stood drinking root beers.

"You boys have done your act. One of you take this little lady to Mercy Hospital. Use my car." Meacham scanned the line of onlookers. "And one of you pull her plane off the runway." He gave directions and keys to Slim as they hurriedly left.

❧

She paced the halls of the hospital's emergency area, then asked about Johnny again. The nurse shook her head. "Miss, as soon as we know, you'll know. No, you can't go in yet."

After what seemed like agonizing days, but was only an hour later, the doctor told her she could see him, but warned her he was still unconscious.

"What's wrong? Will he get better soon?"

"I'll answer the last question first. He's strong and will mend quickly. As to your first question, he sustained many bruises, a deep cut at the back of his head, scrapes on his right side, and broken ribs. I've bandaged him and given him something to make him sleep. He'll wake up in about two hours."

As soon as she reached his bedside, her heart sank. His face was white, and he had dark circles beneath his eyes. He looked so vulnerable and helpless. The bandages wrapped around his head made him look like pictures of war casualties. She didn't see a pulse in his neck. *They didn't tell me the truth. He's dying!* Alarm and anger shook her. *God, don't let him die.*

She stormed out of the room and grabbed the first person she saw wearing white. "Do something! This man is dying!" She pulled the tall, thin nurse into Johnny's room.

The nurse lifted his wrist and felt his pulse, touched his neck, picked up his chart, and shook her head at Meredith. "He's not dying! In fact, he's doing just fine."

"You call this fine?" Meredith choked back sobs. "Look at him."

The nurse gently guided her to a chair beside the bed. "Calm yourself, or you'll have to sit in the waiting room." Meredith meekly sat. "Would you like something to help you relax?"

Meredith shook her head. "No. I'm all right." The nurse left, and she sat by Johnny's bed while tears she could not stop slowly slid down her cheeks.

What's the matter with me? she thought. She felt a profound sense of loss, a deep emptiness. She'd walked away from Johnny and forced herself to believe she didn't need him. But this emptiness was more than just missing him. It went much deeper and was something that had been there for a long, long time, a void that yearned to be filled.

I've got everything I wanted. I make my own plans, I have my own plane, a career, and enough saved up to start my school. So what's missing? I didn't want friends, or lovers. Is that it? Are friendship and love that important?

Johnny stirred, rustling the bed sheets, and she watched carefully for any other movement. He lay still, barely breathing. Her eyes blurred and she caught a vision of herself, standing off in a corner alone with her aeroplane, looking out onto a world of couples in love, families, and fellowship she'd never have. It was as if she was behind an invisible wall she'd erected around her. All she had to do was turn on the light, the walls would dissolve, and she'd have it all.

Turn on the light. The vision was tempting, but she wasn't sure she wanted to leave the comfortable lifestyle she'd worked so hard to obtain. Her body stiffened in stunned surprise. *Why, Merry, you coward!* She was startled to realize that what she was feeling was fear. She was afraid she wouldn't fit in, afraid she'd be brushed aside.

Nonsense! she told herself. *You're just imagining things be-*

cause you're overwrought by seeing Johnny in this state. She frowned. *Why is he in San Francisco, anyway?*

His shock of hair fell onto his forehead. She leaned over and brushed it back, but it slipped off the bandage and fell right back over his brows. His eyes were closed, but she envisioned that faraway look he got, as if seeing things no one else could see. His skin rested easily on his cheekbones, and his mouth was softened by the medication that made him relax.

"Johnny Westmore, you're a puzzle," she said softly. "You're in one of the most unstable, crazy businesses there is, yet you're fighting for stability and dignity. You tell me about God, but yet you don't try to push me like everyone else did. You don't fit into my life's plans, yet I can't seem to do without you."

She knew enough about Johnny to know that along with him she'd have to accept God. She thought about that. She had just admitted she couldn't do without Johnny. What about God?

She frowned, remembering her mother and Pearl. She felt as dead inside as they were. *It's true,* she thought. *Something in me died when they did.* A knot of sorrow tied her stomach. Their memory still hurt, even though she'd kept it from her thoughts for years. But the wound was reopened the night she told Johnny about it. *What can I do?* she wondered. *I can't live with this anguish, and I can't seem to push it back anymore.*

She sat with her elbow resting on the bedside table, her chin in her hand, staring at the worn wooden floor, vaguely noticing movement as people passed the open door. She felt alone and empty.

She bowed her head. "I don't deserve Your forgiveness, but, Lord, I need You." A stillness surrounded her, and guilt sliced her heart. "Forgive me, Father, against You only have I sinned, and I repent. I give my heart to You again, and I will trust You forever." Tears coursed down her cheeks as a rising warmth flooded through her. "Thank You," she whispered.

Suddenly she sat bolt upright. Johnny's business! It was very important to him, and he probably had commitments. She left the room, found a phone, and called Los Angeles. Ernie answered, and she told him about the accident.

"Is he all right?" asked Ernie.

"He has a few bruises, broken ribs, and some cuts. But the doctor says he'll be fine. He'll be awake in a couple of hours."

"I'm glad you're there with him," said Ernie.

"So am I," she agreed, unable to stop smiling.

She found the ladies' room, wincing at herself in the mirror while washing her hands. She washed the grime from her face, relieved that Johnny hadn't awakened. Seeing her like this would probably cause a relapse, she thought, scrubbing the dirt from her cheeks. *But he'll revive when he hears I've returned to God.*

She didn't have her purse, but she had a comb in her coverall pocket. She undid the ribbon tied at the back of her neck and pulled the comb through the tangled curls. She took the most unruly hair from the top of her head and tied it at her neck, leaving the curls underneath loose. It gave her a softer, more feminine look.

She leaned closer to the mirror and inspected her freckles. They seemed to pop out more in the sunshine. There was nothing to be done about them, and she had to admit she didn't have the time or inclination to buy powder and paint. She twisted a disobedient curl at her temple into a ringlet, and looked in the mirror to see if the glow on the inside showed on her face.

When she re-entered Johnny's room, she was surprised to see him watching the door as if he expected her. His blue eyes were filled with tenderness.

"I'm sorry we argued when I left Los Angeles," she said, blurting out the first thing that came to her mind.

"Me, too," he said and winced in pain. "What happened? I feel like I've been thrown out of a hot air balloon and trampled by a herd of angry bulls."

"You were saving my life, and you nearly fell off the plane you were standing on."

He closed his eyes. "Your wheel got knocked cockeyed. I had to fix it," he said in a tired voice. He opened his eyes and tried to lift himself on his elbow, but he fell back with a grimace. "Did you land all right?"

"I'm fine!" she said, alarmed at his weakness. "But you're not. You've got to take it easy for a while."

He laid his hand on his tightly bandaged ribs. He felt the bandage on his head. "I got a little banged up out there, didn't I?" He moved his legs. "My legs seem to be okay. I'm getting out of here. I have work to do. Get the doctor for me."

"I called L.A. It's Saturday, and Ernie is taking care of everything. He says come back soon, but get well first."

Johnny took several shallow breaths. "Thanks." He closed his eyes, and she thought he'd gone back to sleep. She pulled the chair to the edge of his bed.

He opened his eyes and reached for her hand. "Thank God you're all right. I was pretty scared there for a while."

"Why did you do it, Johnny? Why did you risk your life to save mine?"

"You really don't know?" He looked up at her through half-closed lids.

"I . . . I thought, well . . ."

He held his eyes open and gazed at her intently. "When you love someone, you're willing to give your life for them," he said. "It's as simple as that."

Meredith couldn't tear her gaze away from the love she saw in his eyes. The air around them seemed charged. The peaceful feeling she'd felt earlier surrounded her like a pool of warm water.

"What I did is a lot less than what God did for you." He observed her closely. "You look different," he said.

She shook her head back and forth, tears welling up in her eyes. "I've pushed God out of my life for so long . . . I thought He didn't care."

"He never stopped caring." He dabbed her cheeks with the corner of the sheet. "And neither will I."

She sniffed and brought her emotions under control. "I know. I've put my life back in God's hands. These are tears of joy."

His smile broadened with relief. "From the moment you touched down at Meacham's field in that audacious purple aeroplane, I knew we were meant to be together. I love you, Merry. I'll always be there for you."

She felt the bond that had grown between them. It was so strong, she wondered how she'd been able to deny it. "I love you, too," she said, and laid her head on his shoulder gently so as not to hurt him. With her heart in her eyes, she looked up at him. "I've never met a man I wanted to share my life with, but nothing is important anymore if you're not there."

Their gazes locked, and he said in a husky voice, "Will you marry me?"

"Yes," she whispered, then sat back smiling at him. "And I know a preacher who'll be glad to officiate, unless he wants to give me away."

"What?" Johnny looked at her, not understanding.

"Remember? My father is an evangelist."

Johnny closed his eyes and heaved a big sigh. "Thank You, Lord."

"Thank You, Lord," agreed Meredith, holding his hand tightly. She'd found the love on the ground that she'd always felt while soaring through the sky. Her soul was finally at rest.

A Letter To Our Readers

Dear Reader:

In order that we might better contribute to your reading enjoyment, we would appreciate your taking a few minutes to respond to the following questions. When completed, please return to the following:

Rebecca Germany, Editor
Heartsong Presents
P.O. Box 719
Uhrichsville, Ohio 44683

1. Did you enjoy reading *Fly Away Home*?
   ❑ Very much. I would like to see more books
      by this author!
   ❑ Moderately
      I would have enjoyed it more if _____

   _____

2. Are you a member of **Heartsong Presents**? ❑Yes ❑No
   If no, where did you purchase this book? _____

   _____

3. What influenced your decision to purchase this
   book? (Check those that apply.)

   ❑ Cover   ❑ Back cover copy

   ❑ Title   ❑ Friends

   ❑ Publicity   ❑ Other_____

4. How would you rate, on a scale from 1 (poor) to 5
   (superior), **Heartsong Presents'** new cover design?_____

5. On a scale from 1 (poor) to 10 (superior), please rate the following elements.

    __Heroine   __Plot

    __Hero   __Inspirational theme

    __Setting   __Secondary characters

6. What settings would you like to see covered in **Heartsong Presents** books?_____

_____

_____

7. What are some inspirational themes you would like to see treated in future books?_____

_____

_____

8. Would you be interested in reading other **Heartsong Presents** titles? ❏ Yes   ❏ No

9. Please check your age range:
   ❏ Under 18   ❏ 18-24   ❏ 25-34
   ❏ 35-45   ❏ 46-55   ❏ Over 55

10. How many hours per week do you read? _____

Name _____

Occupation _____

Address _____

City _____ State _____ Zip _____

Introducing New Authors!

_____ **Nancy Lavo**—*A Change of Heart*—When Laura Wells's father is unable to accompany her on a much anticipated Caribbean cruise, Graham Kirkland agrees to chaperon Laura and her bubbly friend, Kathi. Turbulent waters are ahead as Laura must learn to release her anger toward God. HP133 $2.95

_____ **Phyllis A. Humphrey**—*Flying High*—When Kelly Marsh's job forces her into contact with Steven Barry, the dark, arrogant skydiver, Kelly is immediately skeptical. Kelly can't have fallen in love with Steven, a non-Christian with such a dangerous and frivolous career. Yet, when God touches the most stubborn hearts, miracles can happen. HP142 $2.95

_____ **Peggy Darty**—*Morning Mountain*—Suzanne is confident she'll find a way to keep the family ranch, but she is unprepared to handle the wounded stranger she finds in the hills. His mysterious ways, the wedding ring in his bag, and the way he comes and goes like a shadow can only bring trouble. HP143 $2.95

_____ **Cara McCormack**—*Drewry's Bluff*—When Drewry's uncle promises her in marriage in payment of a gambling debt, she feels she must take matters into her own hands, and quickly! Through an unexpected turn of events, she arrives in Richmond, ready to assume a new identity as nanny to the two young children of wealthy plantation owner and widower Chase Auburn. HP147 $2.95

Send to: **Heartsong Presents** Reader's Service
P.O. Box 719
Uhrichsville, Ohio 44683

Please send me the items checked above. I am enclosing
$_____(please add $1.00 to cover postage and handling per order. OH add 6.25% tax. NJ add 6% tax.).
Send check or money order, no cash or C.O.D.s, please.
 To place a credit card order, call 1-800-847-8270.

NAME _____

ADDRESS _____

CITY/STATE _____ ZIP _____

NEW4

·····Hearts♥ng ·····

HISTORICAL ROMANCE IS CHEAPER BY THE DOZEN!

Any 12 *Heartsong Presents* titles for only $26.95 **

Buy any assortment of twelve *Heartsong Presents* titles and save 25% off of the already discounted price of $2.95 each!

**plus $1.00 shipping and handling per order and sales tax where applicable.

HEARTSONG PRESENTS TITLES AVAILABLE NOW:

__HP 1 TORCH FOR TRINITY, *Colleen L. Reece**
__HP 2 WILDFLOWER HARVEST, *Colleen L. Reece**
__HP 7 CANDLESHINE, *Colleen L. Reece*
__HP 8 DESERT ROSE, *Colleen L. Reece*
__HP 11 RIVER OF FIRE, *Jacquelyn Cook**
__HP 12 COTTONWOOD DREAMS, *Norene Morris**
__HP 15 WHISPERS ON THE WIND, *Maryn Langer*
__HP 16 SILENCE IN THE SAGE, *Colleen L. Reece*
__HP 19 A PLACE TO BELONG, *Janelle Jamison**
__HP 20 SHORES OF PROMISE, *Kate Blackwell**
__HP 23 GONE WEST, *Kathleen Karr*
__HP 24 WHISPERS IN THE WILDERNESS, *Colleen L. Reece*
__HP 27 BEYOND THE SEARCHING RIVER, *Jacquelyn Cook*
__HP 28 DAKOTA DAWN, *Lauraine Snelling*
__HP 31 DREAM SPINNER, *Sally Laity*
__HP 32 THE PROMISED LAND, *Kathleen Karr*
__HP 35 WHEN COMES THE DAWN, *Brenda Bancroft*
__HP 36 THE SURE PROMISE, *JoAnn A. Grote*
__HP 39 RAINBOW HARVEST, *Norene Morris*
__HP 40 PERFECT LOVE, *Janelle Jamison*
__HP 43 VEILED JOY, *Colleen L. Reece*
__HP 44 DAKOTA DREAM, *Lauraine Snelling*
__HP 47 TENDER JOURNEYS, *Janelle Jamison*
__HP 48 SHORES OF DELIVERANCE, *Kate Blackwell*
__HP 51 THE UNFOLDING HEART, *JoAnn A. Grote*
__HP 52 TAPESTRY OF TAMAR, *Colleen L. Reece*
__HP 55 TREASURE OF THE HEART, *JoAnn A. Grote*
__HP 56 A LIGHT IN THE WINDOW, *Janelle Jamison*
__HP 59 EYES OF THE HEART, *Maryn Langer*
__HP 60 MORE THAN CONQUERORS, *Kay Cornelius*
__HP 63 THE WILLING HEART, *Janelle Jamison*
__HP 64 CROWS'-NESTS AND MIRRORS, *Colleen L. Reece*
__HP 67 DAKOTA DUSK, *Lauraine Snelling*
__HP 68 RIVERS RUSHING TO THE SEA, *Jacquelyn Cook*
__HP 71 DESTINY'S ROAD, *Janelle Jamison*
__HP 72 SONG OF CAPTIVITY, *Linda Herring*
__HP 75 MUSIC IN THE MOUNTAINS, *Colleen L. Reece*
__HP 76 HEARTBREAK TRAIL, *VeraLee Wiggins*
__HP 79 AN UNWILLING WARRIOR, *Andrea Shaar**
__HP 80 PROPER INTENTIONS, *Dianne L. Christner**
__HP 83 MARTHA MY OWN, *VeraLee Wiggins*
__HP 84 HEART'S DESIRE, *Paige Winship Dooly*
__HP 87 SIGN OF THE BOW, *Kay Cornelius*
__HP 88 BEYOND TODAY, *Janelle Jamison*

*Temporarily out of stock.

(If ordering from this page, please remember to include it with the order form.)

········Presents········

*Temporarily out of stock.

Great Inspirational Romance at a Great Price!

Heartsong Presents books are inspirational romances in contemporary and historical settings, designed to give you an enjoyable, spirit-lifting reading experience. You can choose from 156 wonderfully written titles from some of today's best authors like Colleen L. Reece, Brenda Bancroft, Janelle Jamison, and many others.

When ordering quantities less than twelve, above titles are $2.95 each.

Heart♥ng Presents
Love Stories Are Rated G!

That's for godly, gratifying, and of course, great! If you love a thrilling love story, but don't appreciate the sordidness of some popular paperback romances, **Heartsong Presents** is for you. In fact, **Heartsong Presents** is the *only inspirational romance book club*, the only one featuring love stories where Christian faith is the primary ingredient in a marriage relationship.

Sign up today to receive your first set of four, never before published Christian romances. Send no money now; you will receive a bill with the first shipment. You may cancel at any time without obligation, and if you aren't completely satisfied with any selection, you may return the books for an immediate refund!

Imagine. . .four new romances every four weeks—two historical, two contemporary—with men and women like you who long to meet the one God has chosen as the love of their lives. . .all for the low price of $9.97 postpaid.

To join, simply complete the coupon below and mail to the address provided. **Heartsong Presents** romances are rated G for another reason: They'll arrive *Godspeed!*